A Christmas Village

Three Christmas Novellas

by

Ann Acton

Liz Adair

Terry Deighton

A Christmas Village
Published by Century Press
496 West Kane Drive
Kanab, UT 84741

ISBN: 978-0-9905027-4-6
Printed in the United States of America
Year of first printing: 2014

The three of us, Ann, Liz and Terry, dedicate this anthology
to our husbands, Scot, Derrill and Al.
Thanks, guys, for your unfailing support.

To Melanie,
Merry Christmas!
Love,
Judy

CONTENTS

Christmas Gift

by

Ann Acton

Ann's Acknowledgements

I'd like to thank my critique group, Bonnie Harris, Tanya Mills, and Christine Thackeray for their support and encouragement, and to Rebecca Barrett for her marathon beta reading. She is as kind as she is thorough. I want to specifically thank critique members, Liz Adair for her baptism-by-fire education in writing and her blind faith and Terry Deighton who edited tirelessly and never threatened to kill me for my inability to use a comma. (Though she probably thought about it.)

Of course none of this would be possible without my wonderful family, whose lack of whining and need for cooked meals makes writing possible. I love you so much. I also want to say thanks to my Dad and Bobbie who were the inspiration for this story and constantly show me the true meaning of kindness, and to Mary Muir who didn't live to see the dream, but started the fire.

Christmas Gift ~ 1

CHRISTMAS IS ABOUT one thing—gifts. You can tell me it's the tinsel and holly or even the feeling of goodwill in the air, but nobody ever jumped up and down because they found goodwill in their stocking.

Gifts are what drive the holiday season. In my house, the brunt of buying those gifts falls to me. I'm happy to do it, but somehow, every year, I run out of month before I run out of shopping. Then I spend the last 48 hours in a panic-induced marathon until I hate every elf and reindeer, but not this year.

Before the Thanksgiving turkey had even been put away, I jumped into shopping mode. I pored over each and every ad, braved stores at four a.m. to get the best deals, and managed to find the perfect gift for everyone on my list down to the perfect paper to wrap it all in.

With a whole week left until the big day, I felt

victorious. I went to the mall and smugly picked up nothing more than dry cleaning. Then I lounged on a bench and watched the crazed shoppers while I sipped an eggnog milkshake. I was usually right there with them, the biggest nut in the whole fruitcake. Today, with my shopping and wrapping done, I could stop and savor Christmas a little.

I'd never taken the time to notice the elaborate decorations before. Lush garlands and beautiful ornaments surrounded the mini north pole in the center of the mall. Exquisite—a regular Christmas wonderland. I reveled in beauty and tranquility as I slurped the last of my shake.

I sighed. The gloating would have to end. After a morning of snowball fights with the neighborhood kids, Becky and Jeremy would want lunch soon. I stood to toss my cup into the trash and heard the only voice that could end my Christmas glee.

"Amanda Grover, is that you?" Cathleen's loud squawk echoed across the mall. Her husband worked at the same computer company as mine, though he ranked way higher up the food chain than Ethan.

I tried to form a convincing smile. "Cathleen, what a surprise." I felt like a fraud, but I didn't want to be rude. Cathleen had somehow adopted me as one of her "friends" during the last few months. Ethan hadn't been with the company long and couldn't afford enemies, especially those with the pull of Cathleen's husband.

She grabbed me into an awkward hug. Then in a singsong voice said, "Careful of my manicure, dear, I just got it done." Stepping back, she grabbed my hand and clucked her tongue. "These could use a mani for sure. No one wants to have lumberjack hands at the company party. Let me give you the number of my gal."

This is why I loathed Cathleen. She could insult you and make it seem like conversation. I took the number and resolved not to let even Cathleen ruin the joy of my holiday success. "Doing some last minute shopping?"

"Oh, heavens, no, darling. I wrapped that up long ago. I refuse to be one of these people rushing around the mall in a panic at the last minute."

"I know. What—"

"I always finish by the end of October." She gave me a consoling squeeze. "Don't worry dear. You'll do better next year."

"But I'm not—"

"My goodness, look at the time." She glanced at her expensive looking watch. "I still have to get my dress and lay out Jerry's clothes for him. I'll see you tonight at the party. Good luck with your shopping." She shot a cringing glance at my hands again. "And do try to squeeze in some time for that manicure."

Before I could respond, she had already stridden off down the mall.

I picked up my dry cleaning, my mood black and ugly. *That woman*, I fumed all the way back through the decorated hallways. They seemed cheap and gaudy now. I reached the parking lot and unlocked my car. "That woman," I repeated aloud, throwing my clothes into the backseat and climbing behind the wheel. I went over the conversation in my mind, trying to figure out how I could have changed the outcome but to no avail.

It wasn't until I pulled onto the freeway that I remembered my dress for the party lay in the heap of dry cleaning on the back seat and would now be wrinkled.

Cathleen wouldn't be wrinkled, but, then again, she probably had a "gal" for that, too. She'd look perfect with her designer dress and expertly teased hair. I turned into the driveway and saw Ethan's car. He wasn't due home for a few more hours.

I waved to the kids, still in the middle of a raging snowball war, and got out to retrieve the dry cleaning from the back seat. My mind still spun. Of course Cathleen finished her shopping by October. Her husband made three times what Ethan did. Cathleen never had to live paycheck to paycheck or get up early to chase a deal. Money made everything easier.

"Hi, Mommy." My five year old, Becky, stood in front of me. She looked adorable in her pink snowsuit. My black mood lifted a bit.

"Hi, Sweetie. Are you having fun?" Her little cheeks and the tip of her nose were red from the cold.

"Yes, but I'm starving. What's for lunch?"

"How about mac and cheese?"

Becky threw her arms around me. "Yay." She pressed her little body against my legs, encasing the clothes between us, which I knew meant more wrinkles, but it was worth it.

A snowball hit the trunk of the car, sending splatters of snow everywhere. Becky ran back to the game, and I tried to shake the drops of snow off the garment bag as best I could. I hoped I could get the bag off without getting water spots on my dress, too.

Ethan met me at the door as a barrage of snowballs exploded around me. He slipped an arm around my waist and tugged me into the warmth of the house. "The natives are restless, honey. They're starting to attack." He pulled me into his arms. "Don't worry, I'll protect you."

I sank into his embrace, enjoying the warmth and smell of him. "This is a nice surprise, but why are you home so early?"

"I'm working with Jerry right now on a special project. There wasn't much going on today, so he let us all leave early because of the party tonight."

The mention of Cathleen's husband rekindled my frustration. Jerry could really help Ethan's career, but dealing with that woman seemed a heavy price to pay for it. I headed toward the bedroom to put away the dry cleaning. "What kind of a special project?"

Ethan followed. "I got pulled onto it this week, so I'm still getting up to speed, but we're designing software that will track Christmas spending habits for retailers. It's actually pretty cool. I'll have Jerry tell you more about it tonight if you want. We're sitting at his table."

"Oh, good, an entire night of Cathleen. Merry Christmas to me." I carefully lifted the splattered bag and put the clothes into the closet, separating my dress from the stack and examining the damage.

Ethan came up behind me and rubbed my shoulders. "I know Cathleen is a handful, but she likes you. You know working with Jerry could be a great opportunity for me."

I hung the dress on the closet door. "Why do you think I haven't killed her yet?"

Ethan smiled and pulled me into another kiss. This time, I let myself get swept up in the moment. A chorus of giggles met us from the hallway as Becky and her older brother stood staring at us in dripping snowsuits.

I pointed to the laundry room. "Snowsuits into the dryer, please."

Ethan gave me a peck on the lips. "I'll start lunch," he said and herded the kids toward the laundry room.

I surveyed the dress with a sigh. With an entire night of Cathleen ahead of me, a rumpled dress would be the least of my problems.

Christmas Gift ~ 2

I USUALLY LOVE Christmas parties, but I couldn't shake the feeling of dread as I took my seat. Although she hadn't showed yet, I knew Cathleen and her sharpened tongue were slated to arrive at any moment.

Ethan leaned over and whispered, "That's not a very festive face. Santa's watching; you know."

I glared at him. "Santa should bring me a convertible for the torture I'm about to go through."

"I wouldn't necessarily call an evening out with me torture." He gave me a sly smile and arched an eyebrow. "I'll have you know I'm considered quite a catch."

His smile was contagious. "I'm sorry. You're right. We haven't been out alone in forever, and you look handsome tonight." I leaned in for a quick kiss.

No more moping. Ethan's company had booked a beautiful venue and decorated it to the hilt. I would be positive and cheerful and simply focus all my energy on my handsome husband. Not even Cathleen would crush my Christmas spirit.

The opening remarks came and went. No Cathleen. The salads were served and then taken away with still no sign of Cathleen or Jerry. The power of positive thinking, I concluded. The universe had rewarded me for my determination to be merry.

As waiters served the main course, I started to feel giddy, and then I heard her from the doorway. Her voice seemed to carry across the universe. My once delicious beef Wellington turned to a rock in my stomach.

Jerry sat first as Cathleen greeted everyone on her way to the table. Ethan took my hand as a sign of support or perhaps a warning to be nice. He should know I'd take one for the team. Hadn't I always sacrificed for his career? When we were first married, we'd lived in an apartment so small I could literally touch the kitchen table from our bedroom. I spent late nights at a job I disliked for years to help pay the bills. We even put off starting a family until he settled into a decent position. Ethan and I were a team, and I would play my part.

Cathleen slid into the chair next to me, her perfume heavy and sweet. "Amanda, don't you look nice. I hardly recognize you out of jeans and a tee-shirt."

I hoped my face didn't betray my annoyance. "Thank you. You look lovely, as always."

At least that statement didn't smack of insincerity. Cathleen was a beautiful woman, and her looks hadn't dimmed with age. The slight silver in her hair only added a regal quality. Dressed in a perfectly tailored, emerald gown, she looked stunning.

It made me a little jealous, but I consoled myself by focusing on the slight puffiness around her eyes. Secretly, I wondered how many injections she'd endured to look that good. Probably the reason they were so late, she'd had a little nip and tuck delay.

"Oh, honey." She reached for my hand and made a face. "I see that you didn't fit that manicure in." As she released her grip, I slid my hands under the table.

Cathleen wagged a perfectly polished finger at me. "Don't you worry about it. Being a mother is a sacrifice worth looking less than perfect for."

What exactly did that mean? I opened my mouth to respond, but Ethan interrupted. "Jerry, I told Amanda you would explain the project we're working on. I mentioned it to her earlier, but I'm afraid I'm still getting up to speed."

Jerry filled me in, and I had a reprieve from Cathleen throughout the rest of dinner. The software sounded amazing. I could see how useful it would be for retailers. I could also see that Ethan's work had impressed him. Cathleen looked bored, but she didn't interrupt.

I almost believed the evening wouldn't be so bad, but as the dessert cart rolled around, Jerry's phone rang. I saw a shadow pass across Cathleen's features as he answered.

She turned to me. "Always something left undone. Jerry's never learned to enjoy a good party."

He gave Cathleen a pointed look. "Can you hold on a second, Daniel? I need to go into the hallway. It's too loud in here." He rose and started to walk out of the room. He got past the table and called back, "Ethan, you'd better come, too. It looks like some of the projections are coming in differently than we anticipated. I might need your input."

Ethan gave me an apologetic smile and followed Jerry into the hallway. Trying not to grimace, I turned my attention to the dessert cart. I choose a decadent, chocolate torte for myself and one for Ethan.

Cathleen waved off the waiter.

"You're not going to get anything?"

"Oh no, dear, I gave up dessert years ago." She eyed the rich chocolate on my plate. "I admire your enthusiasm, though, especially with your body type." She fluffed her hair. "Now remind me. You have two children? Is that right?"

I pulled at my dress self consciously. "Yes, Becky's five, and Jeremy will turn nine this spring."

"How wonderful. I bet they're excited for Christmas."

This was exactly the topic I had been waiting for. If I could steer the conversation my way, I could set Cathleen straight about my triumphant holiday shopping, maybe even gloat a little bit. "Oh, yes." I answered. "They've been filling out their Christmas lists since October." I took a bite of my dessert and waited for her to take the bait.

Cathleen frowned. "Oh that's hard. It's so difficult to teach them that Christmas is about giving to others and not greed. Hopefully, they'll grow out of it soon, but you have to set the standard."

Wait. What happened here? I'm supposed to be gloating now, and instead my kids are being pegged as materialistic. I swallowed quickly, so I could defend them. "The kids aren't greedy. They—"

"Oh, I know, it's fun to see them so excited about presents now, but mark my word, those kids will never learn the true meaning of Christmas unless they start giving back."

The conversation had completely gone south.

Cathleen continued. "With our daughter, Mandy, I had to practice tough love. I started serving with her at the shelter on Christmas Eve whether she liked it or not. Oh mercy, she fought me like a bear for the first three years, but she came around. Now she's in medical school, still giving back."

"That's wonderful," I said, mentally willing one of the many Christmas trees that decorated the room to fall on Cathleen's head. I took another bite of dessert and half listened as Cathleen droned on about her perfect daughter.

"She's a giver that one. In fact, she won't be able to make it home this year with finals and work and all. It's very disappointing, but we all have to sacrifice." Cathleen's bragging stopped suddenly. "Oh,

I have a brilliant idea. You and the children can join me this year at the shelter."

She had my attention now. "I don't know," I stammered. "The kids are still a little young for something like that."

"Nonsense. It'll be great for them." Cathleen clapped her hands together. "We'll meet there on Christmas Eve. It'll make this Christmas memorable."

On Christmas Eve we were supposed to go ice skating and out to dinner with the kids not ladle soup for the homeless. How did this happen? "Cathleen, I don't know if the children—"

"Now, honey, you can't back down. They'll fight the idea, but you said it yourself, they desperately need to learn the true spirit of giving."

I didn't remember saying anything like that. "I really think—"

"Don't worry, dear Amanda. I don't judge you. It takes a village to raise a child. I'm only too happy to help. Now, I've got to run to the little girls' room. We'll iron out the details when I get back." She placed a manicured hand on my arm and gave it a little squeeze. Then she headed for the restroom, loudly chatting with several people on her way.

Not long after, Ethan returned to the table alone. "I got back as soon as I could. How are you faring?" His eyes lit up at his dessert, and he grabbed a fork.

I narrowed my eyes. "Oh, I'm great. Somehow I agreed for our family to work with Cathleen at the homeless shelter on Christmas Eve, but other than that, I'm fine."

Ethan's fork stopped short, inches from his mouth. "You did what? I thought we were taking the kids skating on Christmas Eve?"

"We were...are. I don't know what happened. One minute we were talking about the kids, and the next minute, the shelter became the only way to save them. You have to help me fix this. Tell Cathleen we can't make it."

He shook his head. "No way."

"Ethan!"

"I can't do it, Amanda. Jerry told me this project could bring in high revenues for the company. He wants me to take a bigger role. I'm not going to be the one that looks like a heartless louse to his wife."

"So you're okay with spending Christmas Eve spooning up mashed potatoes for the unwashed masses?"

He took another bite of the torte. "Maybe it's a good thing."

I stared at him in disbelief.

"Teaching the kids about service will be a good lesson. We'll still go skating and to dinner. We'll just add serving at the shelter to the list. I look at this as a win-win."

I scowled at him and took his dessert away.

"It'll be okay." He kissed my cheek and stole the plate back.

I sat brooding. I should have told Cathleen I could live with my kids being heartless brats. Only hours ago, I'd thought a whole evening with her would be the worst thing in the world. Now, I had signed up for another dose with a trip to a dirty homeless shelter as a bonus. Why can I never learn to quit while I'm ahead?

Christmas Gift ~ 3

THE KIDS, AS I expected, weren't thrilled with the idea of serving at the shelter. Becky seemed apprehensive about the people, but Jeremy was near mutiny. "I don't understand why we have to do this," he whined as we drove from the skating rink on Christmas Eve.

"Because Christmas is all about being kind," I said, but in my mind I answered, *because I have no spine, and dealing with Cathleen is like reasoning with a steamroller.*

"Can't we just be kind to people in our neighborhood?" Jeremy said.

What a great idea. I could have used this kid around last night when I sold out our Christmas Eve. I had to be positive. After all, I'd gotten us into this mess. "These people are having a hard time. We should help them if we can. Besides, think about all the bonus points you'll earn with Santa."

"But my legs hurt, and I'm starving," Jeremy said.

"Me too, mommy," Becky agreed.

I had nothing to offer since, after two hours of skating, I felt the same way.

Ethan must have sensed my determination wavering and decided to lend a hand. "Look, guys, we don't have to stay very long, and when we're done, we can go to dinner wherever you want."

"Even Pizza Palace?" Jeremy asked without hesitation.

Ethan looked to me. I thought about the medieval nightmare of whizzing games and bad pizza, but Jeremy loved it. I cringed but nodded.

"Pizza Palace it is," Ethan said.

Jeremy still didn't look happy, but I'd take a mopey face over outright rebellion.

Becky leaned forward. "Can we go to the store afterward? I have one more present to buy, and I brought my piggy bank." She jiggled the ceramic pig filled with quarters and dimes she'd been saving. She'd even been asking for jobs around the house to earn extra quarters.

"Of course we can," I said.

We pulled up to the address Cathleen had given us. It matched a three story brick building in a part of town I'd never really been to. We parked the car and got out hesitantly. Everything looked dirty and broken. A few people walked along the street. Each of them looked as ragged as the surrounding buildings. I

16

couldn't shake the feeling that we would come back to find our car without any tires.

I hid Becky's piggy bank under the seat, so no one would break the windows to get to her few coins. As we walked around the corner, I wondered if coming had been a mistake. This place seemed dangerous and depressing. I didn't feel like there could be anything my kids could learn here except maybe the importance of a tetanus shot.

We neared the entrance of the building. The stark difference in the atmosphere as we entered took me by surprise. Hundreds of paper snowflakes decorated clean, bright, glass doors and windows. Red and green paper chains and twinkle lights looked happy and inviting strung over the bushes and a sign that read "Community Center."

Inside, children's drawings and brightly lit garlands adorned the walls. Some of the decorations were well worn, but the overall effect was one of celebration. To our left sat an enormous tree covered in homemade ornaments and more twinkling lights. Next to it, a piano with a red runner across its top merrily played "Jingle Bells" as people gathered around to sing.

I looked around. A few of the people looked as I'd suspected, dressed in mismatched, dirty clothes, but most seemed to be families—not that much different from my own. I squeezed Ethan's hand, thankful for the blessings we enjoyed.

A delicious smell wafted from the lunchroom-style kitchen in front of us, and all around the room, men were setting up long tables and folding chairs from a large closet.

A woman with ebony skin and short, silver-touched hair approached us with a bright smile. "Welcome to Springfield Community Center. I'm Dorothy Boyle, but most people around here call me Dottie. I'm so glad you could join us for our Christmas feast."

I blushed. "Oh, we just came to help. We're friends of Cathleen Goodman."

Dottie nodded. Cathleen is one of our more dedicated volunteers. She's over at the piano right now." I studied the group gathered near the tree and realized that the animated figure playing lively Christmas tunes on the piano was Cathleen. I looked at Ethan in amazement.

"What should we do first?" he asked Dottie.

"Well, if you don't mind, the men could use a couple strong helpers to set up the tables and chairs over there."

Ethan took Jeremy by the hand. "We're on it."

She looked to me. "How are you with a potato peeler?"

"I'm the youngest of six children. I'm practically a professional."

"Excellent." She bent down to Becky. "And for you, young lady, I have a special job. Do you think you could help me with it?"

Becky nodded timidly.

"Oh, good, because I need someone just your size to help me finish decorating the tables."

Becky looked to me for permission. I nodded, and she took Dottie's hand.

"Just go to the kitchen," she said, pointing to the back. "They'll get you started. Folks around here are always happy to see an expert potato peeler."

I went through the doors in the direction she pointed and found a flurry of activity. Pots boiled, producing the delicious aromas that drifted through the center. Fresh rolls had been set on the counter to rise, and a number of turkeys were being checked and basted in the large ovens that lined the wall.

I turned in the direction of a pretty, petite blonde sitting beside a mound of potatoes. She looked around my age, dressed in a simple sweater and jeans.

"Hi," I said. "I'm Amanda. Dottie sent me back to help with the peeling. Do you have room for one more?"

The woman smiled up at me. "Heavens yes, there's a mountain of spuds here, and, so far, only my two hands to conquer them. There's a peeler on the table there. Help yourself."

I easily located the peeler and returned to find the woman had set up a chair and a bucket for the peels for me. She wiped her hands on a dishtowel then reached out to shake my hand. "I'm Erin. Welcome to the pit."

"Nice to meet you," I said. "Happy to be here." It surprised me to find the statement true. This place had a vibrancy and life I hadn't expected. I picked up a potato and pulled the blade across it.

"Do you have children?" she asked.

"Two." I pointed out the open kitchen doors. "Jeremy's there in the blue jacket with his father, and Becky is..." I paused to locate her. She and Dottie were placing decorations on the tables with some other little girls, who looked about her age. "There." I pointed her out.

"So cute," Erin said. "I love the pigtails."

"Thanks. I keep telling myself she'll grow out of them soon, so I put them in every chance I get."

Erin placed another potato on the growing pile. "It happens too fast. I have three. Jamie and Karen." She pointed toward two girls near the piano. One looked around eleven and the other a little younger. They were nearly carbon copies of their mother. "My youngest, Sophia, is next to your Becky—also with pigtails and for the same reason."

An adorable brunette stood next to Becky. Both of them were giggling at something Dottie told them.

I looked around at my family. Ethan and Jeremy worked side by side with determined purpose while Becky helped Erin's daughter carefully place decorations on each table. I felt so proud of my little family. Maybe this experience would be good for the kids. My heart felt a little lighter.

"You know, Erin, I have to confess. I didn't really expect it to be so happy here. I imagined a bunch of dirty, toothless, sad people, milling around and waiting for me to ladle soup. This place is nothing like that. It's bright and alive and really amazing. How long have you been bringing your family here to volunteer?"

Erin got a strange expression on her face. Then she smiled and looked at me kindly. "Since we started living here six months ago."

My face flamed. "I'm so sorry," I stammered. "I just assumed..."

Erin was laughing now. "Don't worry about it. And don't think we don't have our toothless wrecks around here. See that guy?" She pointed to an old man with wild, grey hair and a trench coat. "That's Frank. He's always losing his dentures, and the kids go crazy when he doesn't put them in."

"You must think I'm an idiot."

Her eyes held nothing but amusement. "No, I'm flattered that the last year hasn't made me look like I feel. The recession has been hard on everyone, especially folks around this neighborhood. There aren't enough jobs to go around. My husband couldn't handle it. He took off one morning without even a goodbye."

"I'm so sorry."

She shrugged. "Things were up and down with us before. After three months without work, I guess he figured we were better off apart. It got pretty bleak for me and the girls after he left, but then I met this wonderful woman named Cathleen in the grocery store."

My ears perked up. "Did you say Cathleen?" I gestured toward the piano. "That Cathleen?"

Erin nodded. "She saw me crying in front of the milk aisle. I'd lost a quarter somewhere between home and the store, and I couldn't afford the gallon of milk I needed to buy. I guess it was my last straw." Erin looked at the floor and shook her head. Then she laughed. "It's embarrassing to admit now, but I had a particularly public meltdown right in front of the dairy case. Cathleen came along and saw me sobbing next to the yogurt. She bought us a whole cart full of groceries. It mortified me to get charity from a stranger, but she wouldn't take no for an answer."

Well, at least the pushy part seemed like the Cathleen I knew.

"She told me about this place. It was heaven-sent since we were about to be evicted. Our family has a nice room of our own here, and we share a communal bathroom and dining area. They even have computer classes in the evening, so I'm working to get certified. It's been an amazing blessing for our family." She leaned in and put a hand to her mouth conspiratorially. "I wouldn't mind my own bathroom again, though. That's for sure."

Another woman stepped over and took the potatoes we'd peeled to cut them up. I felt relieved for the interruption since I had no idea what to say.

Thankfully, Erin changed the subject to kids and schools. We fell back into an easy conversation until the potato pile dwindled, and our sides ached from laughing.

Ethan poked his head into the kitchen as we finished the last spuds. "How's it going in here?"

"Great," I said. "We've conquered the biggest mountain of potatoes on the West Coast. I have committed to nothing but rice until New Year's."

He looked at the huge pots on the stove. "I don't blame you. I thought Jeremy and I had the heavy lifting, but I guess we were slacking." He helped me to my feet. "Did you see that your daughter has a new best friend for life?"

I peeked out the door to see Becky walking hand in hand with Sophia toward the Christmas tree.

"Honey, this is Erin." I pointed to my comrade in arms. "Becky's new Siamese twin is her daughter, Sophia."

Ethan shook her hand. Then he turned back to me. "Oh, I almost forgot. Jeremy asked me if he could invite a friend to dinner. I told him I thought it would be alright."

I shrugged. "I don't see any harm in that if his parents don't mind. It is Christmas Eve, though."

"After all that peeling, you're not staying for dinner?" Erin asked.

"I wish I could, but I promised Pizza Palace."

"Yikes," she said with a grimace. "Pizza Palace is the worst. The food is terrible."

"Yes, but don't forget there are lots of noisy games and crying kids everywhere to make up for it."

She patted my shoulder. "You have my condolences. If you survive, maybe we can get the girls together sometime next week for a play date?"

"That's a great idea. Then maybe they won't hate us for separating them tonight."

Ethan pulled his cell phone out. "Give me your number, and I'll put it in my phone."

"Just call the shelter and ask for Erin. I'm the only one by that name here, so they'll come and get me."

Ethan's face went red.

Erin gave me an energetic hug. "Thanks so much for all the help. I'd better go sing some carols with the girls before dinner. It really was nice meeting you both."

I waved as she disappeared through the swinging doors.

Ethan looked stunned. "She lives here? I feel so stupid. She looks so..."

"Normal? I know. It's pretty incredible to think that her life probably looked a lot like ours not that long ago. I hate to admit it, but Cathleen might be right about coming here."

He put his arm around my shoulders, and we walked out into the dining hall to find the kids.

"You know what's even more incredible?" I said. "She feels sorry for *me*. I got sympathy from a woman who lives in a homeless shelter."

"She's very kind."

I looked around at the decorations and laughter, amazed at how sad I felt about leaving. "No," I said with a sigh. "Pizza Palace is just a really rotten place."

Christmas Gift ~ 4

THIS NIGHT AT the shelter had worked out so much better than I had imagined it. We'd done something good, made some new friends, and I hadn't had one conversation with Cathleen. My self esteem had reached its peak. If we could get out before I had to admit to Cathleen she was right, even finishing the evening at Pizza Palace would be okay.

Ethan went to pry Becky away from Sophia, and I waved Jeremy over. "Did you have fun?"

Jeremy shrugged. "I guess so. I mean it wasn't horrible. Are we leaving?"

I noticed a strange, middle-aged man quite close to us. His clothes were worn and heavily stained. His dark hair hung in long, unkempt twists that mixed with his bushy beard, and he smelled of stale alcohol.

"Pizza Palace here we come," I said with fake enthusiasm. "Who did you want to take with us? If it's Spencer, we'll need to make sure we give his grandma a heads up before we drive all the way over there. They may not let him come on Christmas Eve."

"It's not Spencer," Jeremy said.

I looked around for Ethan. The tattered man still lingered a little too close for my comfort. I put myself physically in between my son and the stranger but tried to keep the conversation casual, so Jeremy wouldn't be scared. "Not Spencer? Who then? Jared?"

"Glen."

"Glen?" I searched my memory, trying to remember a Glen on Jeremy's baseball team or from cub scouts. I drew a blank.

"Honey, I don't think I know Glen. Is he a friend from school?" I felt distracted by the man, who kept getting closer and seemed way too interested in our conversation. Maybe this wouldn't be such a great experience for our family. The man nervously stood looking at us. My hands shook, but I tried to keep my voice strong and clear. "Can I help you?"

"Mom!" Jeremy tried to push from behind me.

"Not now, honey. Mommy's handling something." I stared the man down. His eyes slid to the ground, and he started to walk away.

"You're so embarrassing," Jeremy muttered.

I took a step back, unsure what I'd done that could possibly be embarrassing. Didn't this ungrateful kid realize I'd saved him?

Jeremy pushed around me then ran up and grabbed the bearded stranger by the coat. "Mom, *this* is Glen."

I couldn't do anything but stare, first at the stranger and then at my son, waiting for a more rational explanation.

"Jeremy," I began, trying to find a way out, "We don't..."

"Come on, Mom, he's never been to Pizza Palace, and you already said I could bring someone."

I froze. This couldn't happen. I could not drive around town with some strange, dirty, homeless man. He looked and smelled like he hadn't bathed in months. And besides that, putting him in the car with my children definitely didn't feel safe. Who knew what he might do? It would be rude to tell Glen he couldn't come, but should I sacrifice our lives because I didn't want to offend a possible serial killer? I searched desperately for Ethan. He could fix this. He had to fix this.

Cathleen's voice interrupted my full blown panic attack. "I hope you weren't planning to sneak out without saying goodbye."

For once, I felt truly thankful to see her. I threw my arms around her neck, drawing her into a big hug. Shock and embarrassment, more than affection, fueled my actions. "It's wonderful to see you Cathleen, just wonderful."

She returned my awkward hug, eyeing me warily. Then she stepped back. "I thought you'd never be tough enough to get these kids here tonight, but look at you."

Yes, look at us. I'm clinging to my nemesis like we're soul sisters while my son is getting ready to load Jack the Ripper's grungy cousin into my minivan.

I laughed a strange, pinched laugh. "Oh yeah, we made it all right." I searched the room desperately. Where could Ethan have disappeared to? I had reached my meltdown point, and Chernobyl status loomed in the near future.

"Are you all right, dear?" Cathleen said. "You look a little, well, I don't want to say it, but–crazy."

I laughed my strained laugh again, probably confirming her thoughts. "I um, I have a..." *Horrible problem*, I wanted to scream. *A problem that is all your fault.* Then I pictured myself wrapping my hands around her neck and choking her savagely.

Luckily, Ethan arrived with a tearful Becky. "Just a headache," I said, regaining my composure now that Ethan would save the situation. The fact that Cathleen usually caused me pain in another region could be addressed later.

Ethan looked unnerved, probably due to my sweaty face and wild eyes. He turned his attention to Cathleen. "Thanks so much for telling us about this place. We had a great time."

"Had? Are you all leaving before dinner? Darling, that's the best part."

Ethan kept giving me strange glances and finally seemed to notice Glen standing next to Jeremy. "We promised the kids we'd go to Pizza Palace. I had to tell Becky she could take Sophia, too, or we'd never get out the door." He turned to me. "I already asked Erin. She's fine with it. She went to get Sophia's coat."

Jeremy stomped his foot. "But now there isn't room for Glen."

"Who's Glen?" Ethan said.

The man edged forward nervously. "I'm Glen." He fidgeted with his hands and looked down at his shoes.

Ethan looked totally confused and turned to me for an explanation.

I had nothing to offer. Happy for the space issue coming up, I figured we could use it in our favor to avoid taking the dirty man with us. He wouldn't want to make two little adorable girls cry? Would he?

Erin arrived with Sophia.

"We'll have to take Glen another time," I volunteered. *Like when Jeremy turns forty.*

Cathleen shook her head. "I see you didn't plan this out very well." She clucked her tongue at me. "Oh, well it's Christmas, and I'm in a giving mood tonight. I'll come with you to, what is it called again?" She grimaced. "Pizza Palace?"

I nodded mutely.

Cathleen continued. "I'll take the girls with me, so you'll have room. And we may as well take all the girls." She looked at Erin. "It will be my treat, of course. You go get Jamie and Karen, and I'll pick you all up at the front. Come on girls." Cathleen grabbed Sophia and Becky, scooped up her coat, and headed for the door, saying to Becky. "Oh, your silly mommy. Good thing Auntie Cathleen was here."

"All right," Ethan said to me with an apologetic and slightly confused look. "Let's go to Pizza Palace. You wait for Erin to gather her girls, and I'll get..." He paused for a second as if trying to figure out how to categorize our son and his new friend. "... *everyone* settled."

Erin and I stood in the lobby.

She spoke first. "If it makes you feel any better, I've never met that guy before either."

I stared at her.

"So we're all going to Pizza Palace then." She gave a weak fist pump. "Yay." She turned to me with a puzzled expression. "How did that happen?"

"I have no idea. You know Cathleen. She's like a tornado. Before you realize you've been scooped up, you're sitting in Oz surrounded by munchkins." I put my arm around her shoulder. "So are you ready for a night of Christmas Eve fun at Pizza Palace with five kids, the most controlling woman in the world, a possible axe murderer—"

Erin sang out, "And a partridge in a pear tree."

Christmas Gift ~ 5

WE ARRIVED AT Pizza Palace after a very tense drive where Ethan and I tried to learn anything we could about the strange man in the backseat. Glen answered each of our questions with short, one-word answers. I kept looking in the rearview mirror to make sure he wasn't going to kill us, but he barely lifted his head.

Cathleen and Erin pulled up beside us. Karen and Jill piled out, excited for the pizza and games. As the kids led the way toward the building, I started to worry. Pizza Palace sat dark and lifeless. We approached the front door, and my fears were confirmed when I saw a note fluttering in the breeze that read *Closed for Christmas.*

Jeremy's face fell, and his shoulders sank. "No way."

I bent down next to him. "Sorry, honey, I didn't know they were closed tonight."

"But Glen's never been," he insisted.

Glen stood nearby, fidgeting with his hands again and rocking back and forth.

"I'm sorry, but there's nothing I can do."

Cathleen spoke up. "Really, Amanda, you didn't look at the website?" She shook her head. "After dragging us all out here."

I saw Erin cover her mouth to stifle a laugh.

I turned to Cathleen. "I didn't..."

Cathleen patted my arm. "I know, dear, you didn't mean to do this. It's simply bad planning."

"Maybe we should head back to the shelter," I suggested.

Cathleen shook her head. "We've already come all the way out here, and the kids are expecting some fun." She looked around. "There's a restaurant right across the street. We'll make it an adventure."

The kids didn't look like they felt any more enthusiastic about going to the new place than I did.

Erin hooked her arm through mine. Her eyes sparkled with amusement. "Cheer up. We're going on an adventure."

We walked across the street. I could see the neon "Open" sign in the window. We were covered there.

We entered the cramped little lobby and waited to be seated. After a few minutes, Cathleen sighed and called out, "Hell-o-o, we need some help here."

A loud clatter sounded from the back, and then a small, mustachioed gentleman with silver hair appeared from the kitchen. "Welcome to the Wagon Master," he said. "I'm Clint." He looked equally pleased and terrified at the same time. I couldn't tell if it stemmed from being new at this job or because, between my crazed expression and Glen's clothing, we looked like we'd escaped a mental hospital.

"We'd like a large table with a view," Cathleen said.

I glanced around. Dusty, framed cowboy photos and fake wagon wheels decorated the walls over peeling wallpaper. If this place had a view, it would probably be of the parking lot.

Clint tried to direct our party to the back of the empty restaurant, but Cathleen took the lead. She inspected the tables as we walked past them, her nose turned up like she smelled something rotten. Clint stopped in front of a large booth and gestured toward us. Cathleen simply ignored him and started to push two long tables together along the opposite wall.

Clint's little mustache twitched, but he graciously placed a stack of menus on the table Cathleen had chosen and said he would be back with waters. I decided the terror in his eyes must be for Cathleen and wanted to tell him to trust his instincts.

Cathleen acted as hostess, telling each of us where to sit. When she got to Glen, she hesitated as if taking in his appearance for the first time. She shot me a disapproving look, as if I was somehow responsible for such an unkempt guest.

Clint appeared with glasses of water and silverware rolled in white paper napkins on a little tray. Cathleen eyed the glasses. Do you have any bottled water?

Clint shook his head.

Cathleen clicked her tongue. "Do you have any specials?"

"Not tonight. I'm sorry." His mustache twitched again. "I'll just give you all a minute to look over the menu." He practically ran away from the table.

Cathleen sighed. "See why a little planning is so important?" She directed her gaze toward me, and Erin again stifled a giggle.

Did she honestly think I'd planned anything to do with this evening's events? I sat there, wishing we'd stayed at the shelter when Glen spoke up. "Thank you for bringing me."

His eyes reflected genuine gratitude. For the first time I saw him as a man and not a possible threat. I smiled. "You're very welcome. Have you ever been to this place before?"

He shook his head and darted his eyes back to the menu. Apparently that sentence had used up his quota of words.

I looked over the menu. "Becky, they have chicken fingers. Do you want that?"

Becky looked at Sophia, and she nodded. "Yes, we both do."

"Jeremy, did you see something you want? How about a cheeseburger?"

Cathleen snorted. "The only really edible dish on this menu is steak. Do you like steak, Jeremy?"

Jeremy nodded.

"How about you, Glen? Do you want steak, too?" Cathleen asked.

Glen looked at me, and I nodded. "Pick whatever you like."

"Okay," he mumbled.

Cathleen sniffed. "Of course you can have whatever you like, but if you want something worth eating, you should pick the steak."

By the time Clint got back, everyone had decided. Ethan also ordered steak, and all the girls opted for chicken fingers. Erin and I chose cheeseburgers, earning us a sigh from Cathleen.

Clint came back and tried to fill water glasses but only succeeded in pouring water all over Karen. Jill couldn't help but laugh when she screamed, and then they got into an argument. Erin quietly went over to referee and towel off the girls.

We made small talk around the table about the shelter and Christmas plans. Cathleen once again reminded us about her wonderful daughter and her sacrifice to work during the holidays. The conversation kept getting interrupted by loud bangs and clanging coming from the kitchen. A few times there were shouts and even a few curses that sputtered forth, but no food came out. We were all hungry and virtually strangers, so the conversation started to dwindle. The kids grew restless. The adventure portion of this trip seemed to be wearing thin.

"Mommy, I'm hungry," Becky said softly.

"Well, of course you are," Cathleen interrupted. "This is taking forever. Where is that waiter?"

Clint seemed to have made a run for it. I wondered what he could possibly be doing. Other than our party, the restaurant remained empty.

Cathleen scanned the room. I thought she might storm the kitchen, but she turned her attention back to the table. "I wanted to do this later, but it seems we could all use a distraction, so I'll give out some presents."

She pulled a stack of cards out of her purse and passed them first to Erin and her girls and then our kids. She handed a card to me with Ethan's and my names across the envelope. She looked at Glen. "I didn't know you would be joining us, but I have something for you, too. She took a twenty dollar bill out of her purse and gave it to him. "Merry Christmas."

Glen quickly put the money into his pocket. "Thank you," he said, folding his arms tightly across his chest.

Cathleen seemed impatient with our hesitation. "Go ahead. It's Christmas Eve. Open them up." Each of the children's cards contained a twenty dollar bill. Erin's and mine held a gift card for Safeway and enough movie tickets for every member of the family.

"What a thoughtful gift, Cathleen," Erin said. "Thank you so much."

"Yes, thank you," I said. It seemed too easy. Nothing was ever easy with Cathleen, so I waited for the catch.

Cathleen fluffed her hair. "Now we can all go to the theater together, maybe for New Year's."

And there it was. She'd commandeered Christmas Eve, and now she wanted New Year's, too. This woman clung like a wad of chewing gum on a hot sidewalk. The more time I spent with her, the deeper I got tangled up. We were saved a response as Clint finally arrived with the food.

Red-faced and flustered, he placed dishes on the table. He came alone and without a tray, so he could only bring two dishes at a time. The kitchen was located on the other side of the restaurant, so it took an excruciatingly long time for everyone's meal to arrive. By the time he brought them all, sweat dripped from his scarlet face. He wiped at his forehead and nose with his sleeve, making me cringe.

Cathleen had ordered her steak well done. It looked all right, but the other steaks resembled pieces of charcoal. I often joked with Ethan that he ordered his steaks so rare they could graze on his salad, so I could imagine how he felt about this.

My burger came out both burned and stone cold, a truly impressive gastronomical feat. The charcoal patty sat surrounded by a charcoal bun, a blob of condiments, and vegetables that appeared to have been put together by throwing the different parts toward the plate. I looked at Erin's plate and saw my burger's uglier cousin.

The girls at least seemed happy with their chicken strips, but they were pretty dark. I thought at least they might have gotten a decent meal until Karen asked her mother for a knife because she couldn't chew through the tough outer part of the chicken. In short, the worst meal I'd ever seen.

"It's still better than Pizza Palace," Erin whispered to me when she saw the distraught look on my face. She did have a point. I looked around the table as everyone gnawed good-naturedly on their dinner. Only Cathleen and Glen seemed oblivious to the terrible food. I suspected Clint's fear of Cathleen insured her food came out perfectly. Glen apparently had bigger problems than a burnt steak.

Ethan and I picked at our food. I rarely complain at restaurants, but I had hoped to make this meal special for Erin and the girls and even for our newly acquired, though slightly frightening, friend, Glen. I gritted my teeth. Hadn't life been hard enough on them? Could it really be too much to ask for a wonderful meal on Christmas Eve, for crying out loud?

I made up my mind to complain and complain big, even to send back the food to the kitchen. Then Clint came huffing back to the table with a water pitcher. When he got to Cathleen's glass, his hand shook so badly it looked like he had palsy. He looked so pathetic, I lost my nerve. Remembering Karen's near baptism, I passed on the water.

Clint kept his eyes on the floor as if he knew how terrible the food tasted. He never asked about our meal, just busied himself with filling glasses for those brave enough to let him. It took him several trips back and forth to get them all filled, and he kept spilling on the tablecloth, but at least everyone else stayed dry.

"Should we say something to the manager?" I asked Ethan quietly.

He shrugged, looking down at his burnt steak and runny mashed potatoes with lumps.

Everyone finished picking at their plates, and Clint brought the checks. Cathleen insisted on paying for Erin and the girls. "All right ladies, let's load up. Maybe we can all make it back to the shelter in time for pie."

Amazingly, her mood seemed brighter than ever. It might have been because her food hadn't been burned to bits and slung onto the plate or perhaps because she'd been able to strike fear into Clint's heart. She deposited a few bills into the black book that held the check and handed it to me. "You'll make sure the waiter gets this won't you?"

I nodded.

Erin squeezed my shoulder as she put her coat on. Then she bent down close to my ear. "Don't worry. There will be plenty of leftovers at the shelter."

"I'm okay with pie," I said, not wanting to appear as irritated by the lousy service as I felt. "Especially if there's chocolate." Truthfully, this place had ruined my appetite and the happy feeling I'd gained at the shelter. We'd done something good. We'd even brought Glen with us. Karma had let me down.

Cathleen put her arm around Karen and Jill. I waved to Becky as she followed them out the door, hand in hand with Sophia.

"Mom, they have a claw machine," Jeremy said breathlessly.

I dug in my purse and produced five quarters. "That's it. When those are gone, I don't want any whining. Is that clear?"

He nodded as he took the quarters and headed for the lobby. Glen followed him.

Ethan picked up our check. "What should I tip?"

"Honey, I don't really think that we should have been charged for that meal, much less a tip." The earlier resentment I'd felt seemed to triple as I voiced my opinion. "It's called a gratuity because you're showing your gratitude for the service. The only thing I'm grateful for about this meal is that it's over, and no one died—yet."

He looked at his untouched meal. "You have a point. I didn't know whether to eat it or pray over it and toss the ashes around."

I gave a small smile, but it still irritated me that Clint hadn't even offered to fix any of it. "He had to know the food was terrible. I doubt he's really expecting a tip at all."

Ethan shrugged. "It's Christmas Eve. I have to leave something. What would Santa say?" He pulled out his wallet.

While he thumbed out some bills, I glanced over at Jeremy intently trying to win at the claw machine. Glen stood off to the side with Clint. I saw Glen say something to the little host, and then he handed him what looked like the twenty dollars Cathleen had gifted him at dinner.

Clint raised his eyes slowly toward Glen and said something I couldn't make out. Then he shook Glen's hand over and over.

By the time Ethan put the bills into the ticket book and stacked it with Cathleen's offering, the exchange had ended, but it left me more curious than ever about this unusual man.

With their quarters gone, Glen and Jeremy left the restaurant for the car. As Ethan and I walked toward the exit, Clint rushed up to us. His face was flushed, and tears threatened to spill out from behind his large glasses. "I want you to tell your friend how much his tip meant to me." Clint's head dropped, and his eyes looked to the floor. "I know your meal didn't look very good."

Ethan placed a hand on the obviously distraught man's shoulder. "It's fine."

"No." Clint looked up, the tears he'd been struggling with now streaming down his face. "It was terrible. I didn't mean for it to be. The rest of the staff got mad that they had to work tonight, so they left early. I didn't have any place to go, and I really needed the money, so I stayed. I figured not many people would be here tonight, so it wouldn't be too hard."

"So you were trying to run the whole restaurant yourself?" I asked.

Clint gave a soggy nod and wiped at his face with the back of his hand. "I can see now that I really shouldn't have tried. I'm so sorry. Please don't tell my boss."

Ethan passed the man a napkin from a nearby table. "I don't think any one of us would have fared very well in this situation, and don't worry, I've been married for a long time." He took my hand and then winked at Clint. "It's not the first time I've eaten burnt food."

He ignored my glare and ushered me through the door, the little bell singing out our exit. As he followed me, he reached into his pocket and drew out another twenty and handed it to the little man. "Thank you, Clint, and I do hope you have a good Christmas."

Clint just blew his nose loudly into the napkin. "You too," he said, and a fresh stream of tears flowed. "And please tell your friend thank you again for me. You have no idea how much this helps me."

Christmas Gift ~ 6

WHEN WE GOT to the car, we found Jeremy sitting by himself in the back seat. "Where's Glen?" I asked.

"He said he wanted to get out of here."

"So he just left?"

"Yeah, I tried to get him to come back to the shelter with us, but he said he had things he needed to do and walked off."

"Maybe he wanted to hang around till Pizza Palace opens up?" Ethan said.

"How can you make a joke about this?" I asked. "I'm worried about him. Should we go find him?"

"Amanda, I think he'll be okay. Two hours ago, you didn't seem to even want him around, and now you want to spend the rest of Christmas Eve looking for him?"

"I know it seems strange, but I think there is more to him than we know. I hate to think of him being all alone on Christmas Eve." I examined the empty parking lot. I didn't know where to even begin looking.

Ethan patted my arm. "We'll keep an eye out for him on the way to the shelter. If we see him, we'll pull over. Okay?"

I nodded, and Ethan started the car. There were so many things I didn't understand about Glen. I wondered what had happened in his life that brought him to living on the street.

Most of all, I felt confused. Why didn't he keep some of the money? He could have bought food or new clothes. Why would someone give away all they had to a stranger? Clint may be struggling, but even Glen must know that he needed the money more.

We drove back to the shelter, looking carefully down each street in hopes that we would find him, but we never did. We refueled with leftovers and pie at the shelter.

I pulled Erin aside and told her about Glen's disappearing act.

"That's just how some of these people are, Amanda. He'll be okay. Don't worry."

I still wasn't convinced. She told me she'd keep an eye out for him, and that made me feel at least a little better. Becky's eyes were starting to droop, so we decided to call it a night. We scheduled a play date with Sophia for a few days later and got ready to leave.

Cathleen came up to me as we were putting on our coats. "Other than that strange little outing you dragged us on, the night wasn't so bad. Was it?"

I smiled that she thought anyone could make her do anything. "This really has been a wonderful experience," I said without even the smallest hint of sarcasm. "Thank you so much for encouraging our family to come."

She grabbed me in a death grip hug. "That's what friends do. They help each other. If you'd just start listening to me more often, I could help you with all your problems."

I tried not to laugh since listening to Cathleen usually created my biggest problems.

"I'll call you when we set a date for the movies, dear. Have a wonderful Christmas, and don't let Ethan drive like a maniac on the way home."

As we got into the car, I remembered Becky's bank and her last present. I realized the stores would all be closed now and tried to break it as gently to her as possible. "Becky, honey, I'm sorry we forgot to get your last present."

"Oh, that's okay, Mommy. I decided I want to save my money, anyway."

"Oh, really?" I tried not to sound as surprised as I felt, but she'd been so adamant before. "What do you want to save for?"

"For Christmas Eve. I want to do this all again next year."

Christmas Gift ~ 7

THE KIDS BARELY had enough energy left to put out milk and cookies for Santa when we got home. They were exhausted, and I could understand why. My legs were already starting to stiffen from skating earlier. It would take a lot of ibuprofen to get through tomorrow.

After the kids went to sleep, Ethan and I got busy bringing out the last of the presents. I wanted everything perfect for Christmas morning. We opened the attic's pull-down ladder, and I climbed up. As I passed down gifts to Ethan, I couldn't help voicing my thoughts about Glen. "I just don't understand why he gave all that money away."

Ethan stacked the gifts on the floor in the hallway. "He obviously wanted to be kind."

"I understand that, but he didn't keep anything for himself. Even giving some of it to Clint would have been kind. There must have been a million things Glen could have used that money for."

Ethan paused before taking the box I held out to him. "Why is this bothering you so much?"

"I don't know. I'm worried about him. It's cold outside. What if he's cold? I also worry he doesn't have enough food." I picked up another box. "I guess it's also because he gave that money without even knowing any of Clint's story. He didn't care if he deserved it. He gave it because he thought Clint needed it."

"And that's a bad thing?"

I handed Ethan the last present then climbed down. "It's not a bad thing, but it made me wonder if I could ever be that kind."

We picked up the packages and took them to the tree.

You just spent Christmas Eve peeling potatoes at a shelter, and aren't you the founder of the "Take Homeless Man to Dinner" program? You're definitely kind."

I laughed and started to add the packages from his arms to the piles around the tree. "That was actually your son's program, but it's different. I did those things to *appear* kind, not to *be* kind. It's not the same."

"Amanda, you're over-thinking this." He kissed my forehead. "I'm exhausted. Let's go to bed, and we can talk about how heartless and unkind you are in the morning." He grinned at me. "I have a few points I'd really like to bring up."

"Ha ha, you're very clever. Wait till you find elf poop in your stocking. Then we'll see who's bringing up points." I grabbed a bow off one of the gifts and threw it at him. "You go on to bed. I have one more gift I need to get, and then I'll be right in."

After Ethan left, I tugged a huge gift, a chainsaw Ethan had been eyeing for months, out of the hall closet where I'd hidden it. As I pulled at the big box and hefted it toward the living room, I couldn't stop thinking about Glen.

I squeezed between the tree and the fireplace to hide the large package in the back. The prickly branches were harder to manipulate than I'd planned, and a corner of the box bumped the small nativity I'd put up on the hearth for the kids to play with. Wise men and camels scattered everywhere. I put the box down and arranged a few packages around it, and then I turned to grab the fallen figures from the floor and hearth.

I placed the holy family last, first Joseph then Mary. Finally, I picked up the small baby in a manger and nestled him between his parents. Looking at that little scene, I realized Glen was not the only one who'd given all they had to someone who hadn't deserved it.

Christmas Gift ~ 8

I SAT IN the wake of a wrapping paper massacre. My legs ached from yesterday's skating, and my head pounded from the far too little sleep. The energized, little aliens I'd given birth to hardly seemed to notice that they'd gotten up before the sun as they laughed and played with their new loot.

I looked around at the house and decided I'd rather let Ethan take his new chainsaw to it than clean it up. I had avoided my usual last-minute Christmas craziness. I snuggled into my robe and curled up for a well-deserved nap.

As I drifted off, I heard the phone ring. I squinted an eye at the clock on the wall. Eight a.m. Who calls at eight a.m. on Christmas morning? I decided to ignore it and let the machine pick it up.

I curled into a tighter ball and pulled a throw off the back of the couch around me. Whatever anyone needed, it could wait 'til noon. I heard the machine in the kitchen pick up the call.

The unmistakable shrill pitch of Cathleen's voice blared out, but the words were indecipherable from this distance. She probably wanted me to spend New Year's cleaning the sewers to gain character. Well, she was out of luck. If my family was rotten, they could stay that way till July.

Soon the machine quieted, and I returned to my cat nap. I felt myself relaxing into the comfort of the couch. I began to doze. Suddenly, my eyelids were pulled open.

I started awake with a gasp.

"Mommy?" Becky peered into my face. "Mommy, are you awake?"

Awake? Try near seizure.

I pushed her hands off my face. "I am now. What is it?"

"Why is Auntie Cathleen crying?"

"What?" She had my full attention now.

"On the machine. I heard her crying."

Cathleen didn't cry. She demanded and barked. She belittled and slandered, but she never cried. "Are you sure you heard her crying?"

She nodded. "Her voice made that hicuppy sound."

I rubbed a hand over my face and rose from the couch. I stumbled to the kitchen, repressing a yawn and trying to wake up enough to deal with whatever I would hear as I pushed the button on the machine.

The message started. "Amanda...Amanda...are you there? This is Cathleen. Are you up? Probably not; it's early yet. I always get up so early, but that's my way. I get so much done in the mornings."

Thanks, Cathleen, I can always count on you to make sure I know that you do more than I do.

Cathleen's message continued. "Anyway, I hoped you were up and had a minute to talk. I really needed to run something by you. I—" A sob interrupted her comment. "I'm sorry. I'm not usually like this. I really don't—" Another sob interrupted her speech. "It's just without Jerry, I'm—"

At this point in the message, she completely dissolved into choking sobs. "Okay, I'm going to go. I'm not myself today. Forgive me for being such a ninny. Please have a lovely Christmas, and I'll talk to you when I get back."

I stood in the kitchen, staring at the machine long after it clicked off, trying to piece together Cathleen's message. Did she say when she got back? That would imply leaving. And where was Jerry? I groaned. I wanted to curl up and take a nap. I didn't need any Cathleen drama today.

I pushed the erase button. Cathleen probably had lots of friends she could talk to, and she'd probably left already. Hadn't she told me how early she'd been up getting all the things done that I didn't? No way could she get me to leave my comfortable couch. She'd already hijacked my Christmas Eve. She didn't get Christmas Day, too. I stomped to the couch and curled back into my spot.

"Is Auntie Cathleen okay?" Becky asked, looking up from her new doll.

I pulled the blanket back around myself. "I'm sure she's fine."

"So she's done being hiccupy?"

I tried to focus on sleeping. "I guess so."

"Did someone make her some hot chocolate? I always like that when I'm sad."

"I'm sure someone did something like that," I said, but guilt washed over me. I really didn't know if Cathleen had anyone to make her hot chocolate or not. I barely knew anything about the woman except she made my life crazy whenever I gave her the chance.

Well, not today. I had prepared. I had persevered. I had succeeded. I bought everyone the most perfect gifts, and I came in under budget. I had conquered Christmas, and now, I wanted a nap. Cathleen would have to deal with whatever crisis she had created on her own. She'd done nothing but boss and belittle me. She wasn't some sweet widow who needed firewood carried in. She didn't deserve my kindness.

Then I remembered Glen and how he'd treated Clint. He hadn't given him the money because he deserved it. He'd done it because he felt Clint needed it. Shame crept into my heart. A man I hadn't even deemed worthy of riding in my car had shown me a true example of kindness, and I couldn't even follow his example. But why did it have to be Cathleen?

I peeked one eye open. The kids still played with their toys. The television blared out the same cartoon, and Ethan still puttered in his workshop with his new tools. I had erased Cathleen's message. No one would be the wiser if I didn't help her.

My eyes traveled to the nativity directly across from me. I looked at the small baby nestled between his parents, and I knew I couldn't stay home.

"Fine." I threw the blanket to the side and stood, addressing the nativity. "I'm going, but when she's terrible to me, I want you to remember that I got up."

Jeremy looked up from his train set. "Mom, who are you talking to?"

I blushed. "No one."

"Are you having a nervous breakout? Cuz my friend Tony's mom had one, and he told me she had to go to Florida for a while."

"It's a breakdown, honey, a nervous breakdown. And Tony's mom? Wow, I didn't know that." I realized I was babbling, and Jeremy still looked worried.

"I'm fine, honey, I just need to go see Auntie Cathleen." I threw on my clothes and gave Ethan the quick version of the situation.

As I pulled my hair into a ponytail, I thought I may have rushed my answer to Jeremy a little. After all, last night I'd taken a vagrant stranger to dinner, and today I had been arguing with my nativity set. My sanity seemed to be hanging by a thread. A few more outings with Cathleen, and I may need that trip to Florida after all.

Christmas Gift ~ 9

I'D ONLY BEEN to Cathleen's house once before to drop off some paperwork for Ethan. I pulled into the driveway, thankful I remembered how to get there. Cathleen's Lexus was in the driveway, so I assumed she hadn't left yet. I knocked on her front door. No one answered.

A cold wind blew through the trees, whipping my hair around my face and making my eyes water. I hugged my arms around myself and wished I'd had the forethought to bring a hat. I pulled my coat higher up around my neck and pounded on the door. Not long after, I heard someone coming toward the door.

Cathleen's muffled voice called out, "Who is it?"

"It's Amanda," I said through chattering teeth. I readied myself for her scrutiny and criticism when she saw my windswept hair and light coat. Instead, she opened the door and threw her arms around my neck.

"Oh, Amanda, you're here. I prayed someone would come. I'm so alone." She sobbed on my shoulder while I stood awkwardly patting her back. She looked like her usual, not-a-hair-out-of-place self, but her eyes were brimming with tears. The makeup she had skillfully applied that morning had become a black river across her face."

"Cathleen, what on earth is going on? Where's Jerry?"

"Jerry?" A new river of tears started to pour. "He's probably halfway to Mexico with his new girlfriend by now."

Jerry had a girlfriend? I hadn't seen that one coming. I spied a box of tissues near the couch and steered a sobbing Cathleen toward them. After grabbing three or four out, I helped her sit and handed her the Kleenex. She dabbed at her face, which honestly looked like a kind of strange fresco as the makeup smeared in odd swirls of mascara and base.

"Start from the beginning. How do you know Jerry has a girlfriend?"

She took a shuddering breath. "Everything seemed fine until last week. Remember how late we were for the Party? Well, that night I caught him on the phone with her. He denied it, but he's been acting sort of strange since the beginning of the month. That night, I heard him talking on the phone. I came out of the bedroom to show him my dress, and I heard him say, 'Don't worry. She has no idea.' And when he hung up, he said, 'I love you, too.'" She dissolved into a fit of sobbing.

The image of Cathleen's slightly puffed eyes flashed into my brain, and guilt took a stranglehold. How could I have been so cruel at the party? I'd thought the puffiness in her face came from some kind of beauty treatment, but she'd been crying. I'm officially a monster. "Are you sure you didn't misunderstand?"

She blew her nose loudly and shook her head. "He said, 'I love you.' Unless we have a really strange new company policy for our suppliers, I doubt you could label it a business call."

"What did Jerry say about all of this?"

"He told me I'd heard him wrong and to stop acting paranoid. I got so upset I didn't even want to go to the party, but Jerry insisted. I'm surprised you didn't notice I looked like a wreck."

I patted her back and handed her more tissues. "I thought you looked beautiful."

"Oh, Amanda that's sweet, dear, but we both know you don't exactly have an eye for detail."

Ouch. Okay, so the old Cathleen still lurked under this puddle of mascara. I patted her hand and thought about that nativity set. *See I told you she'd be terrible.* I could argue with my subconscious later. I pulled the conversation back to Jerry. "Did anything else happen except the one phone call?"

She shook her head. "Not 'til this morning. The neighbor's dog started barking like crazy and woke me up around five. I leaned over to tell Jerry to take care of it, but he was gone. I looked all over the house, and then I realized his car wasn't in the driveway. He'd snuck out at the crack of dawn without even a note." Cathleen's tears streamed again, and she ran her hands through her hair wildly.

She had started to look a little tribal, but I didn't mention it. "Did you try to call him?"

"That's the worst part. I called ten times with no answer, but then I remembered that last year Jerry kept losing his phone, so I had a GPS installed on it. When I looked it up," she started to sputter and sob. "I...found...him...at the airport. So he's probably long gone by now, basking on a beach somewhere while I cry myself sick on Christmas morning. Who does that? I ask you."

I had to say I didn't think Jerry would. He really didn't seem the type.

"Twenty five years of marriage, and he throws it all away for some blonde."

Had I missed a step? "How do you know she has blonde hair?"

"I don't know, but I can imagine it."

Okay, that seemed like solid logic. I didn't argue, though. While I may not have much of an eye for detail, I can spot a nervous breakdown from a mile away, and Cathleen had reached the finish line.

I handed her another bunch of tissues, and she wiped her face. She'd cried so much now that her makeup had washed off completely. Without the crazy smearing, you could hardly tell she'd been crying. I couldn't believe it. I cry three tears, and I look like I've been hit with a baseball bat. Cathleen nearly fills a bathtub, and within minutes I can't even tell she's been upset. Life is sometimes very unfair.

I stood and urged her to her feet. "Let's go get you some tea."

Cathleen didn't seem to be listening to me, but she followed and sat at the counter as I filled the kettle and put it on the stove. I poked through cupboards, searching for a cup and tea bags. I held up two boxes. "Apple cinnamon or chamomile?"

She looked at me like I'd suggested she graze on the floral arrangement then pointed to the cupboard. "Oh no, dear, the peppermint."

Of course, etiquette clearly dictated peppermint for a nervous breakdown. Apple cinnamon applied only to a midlife crisis. How silly of me. I gritted my teeth and retrieved the tea. I would comfort Cathleen and get her through this, but the nativity set and I were going to have a little talk when I got home.

Cathleen started to rant. "You have no idea how much I sacrificed for that man. I worked in a diner serving the worst coffee and hamburgers for years, so we could pay for his school."

Now she had my attention. "You were a waitress?"

Cathleen nodded. "And a good one, too."

I couldn't picture it at all. Cathleen never listened to a word anyone had to say much less carefully enough to write down an order. I lifted the whistling kettle and poured water into the cups while she continued to reminisce.

"We lived in this little dive apartment over a laundromat. Only 800 square feet and no air conditioning. Sometimes it got so hot in the summer we'd eat ice cream cones three times a day. Jerry called it ice-cream-ditioning. We were so broke, but we were happy." She started to tear up again.

I handed Cathleen a cup. I thought back to my earlier inventions about her life, surprised to see how much we actually had in common.

I noticed a metal bowl on the counter in the corner of the kitchen full of wedding pictures. It seemed out of place in this designer kitchen. "Cathleen." I held up a smiling photo of her and Jerry. "What is all this?"

Cathleen waved her hand at the bowl. "Oh, that. When I tracked Jerry's phone to the airport, I nearly went out of my mind. I tried to call my daughter, but she didn't answer. I remembered she had to work today, so I tried your house. You didn't answer either, and I didn't know where to turn. I got myself all worked up and put a bunch of photos into that bowl."

"Why in the bowl?"

Cathleen looked unashamed. "Tinder, of course."

Confused, I looked closer and noticed the bottle of lighter fluid near the sink. "You were going to light them on fire?"

"Oh, I wanted to burn the whole place down."

My eyes grew huge.

Cathleen dismissed my look with another wave of her hand. "I'll admit, it may have been a bit dramatic. Luckily, we haven't had a match in this house since Jerry stopped smoking five years ago. That slowed me down enough to realize how crazy it all seemed. I went into the bedroom, and I prayed that someone would come and help me."

I picked my cup up and took a small sip. "What happened then?

Cathleen looked up at me with a surprised expression. "Why, you knocked on the door, Amanda. You were my answer."

Gotcha, the little nativity figures seemed to scream at me as I froze, my lips perched over the steaming water. "Cathleen, I—"

"Don't be modest, Amanda. I'm not surprised you're the one who showed up. You are one of the best people I know. I watch you with your beautiful little family. You're such a good mother, so kind and gentle. Sometimes I'm quite jealous of you."

She was jealous of *me*? I put my cup down and looked around. Ashton Kutcher must be hiding in the hallway, waiting to tell me I'd been punked. Just then, I heard a sound at the front door.

"Honey?" Jerry's voice rang out from the entry way.

Cathleen's eyes narrowed, and her face turned to a mask of anger. She plucked a large frying pan off the rack hanging above her head and started to get off the stool.

I grabbed hold of her weapon of choice. "Just go talk to him," I said, prying the cast iron from her fingers.

She turned and went around the little wall separating the rooms. "You have some nerve coming back here when—"

When she paused so suddenly, I have to admit I wondered if Jerry had a pan of his own and had gotten in the first swing. Then I heard multiple voices yell, "Merry Christmas!"

Cathleen started to sputter and wail. I dashed around the corner to see her hugging a young girl with her same auburn hair and Jerry's high cheekbones.

Jerry explained. "Mandy figured out a way to get some time off. She didn't know until a few weeks ago she'd be able to make it, so we decided to surprise you." I thought about that big bowl of "tinder" and the surprise that Jerry might have come back home to.

Cathleen gestured to the girl. "Amanda, this is my daughter, Mandy."

I gave a wave as Cathleen continued. "Amanda just came over this morning to borrow some eggs. Isn't that right, dear?"

I realized she didn't want Jerry to know what a crazy mess she'd been that morning, so I went along with it. "Sorry to interrupt your morning. I forgot all the stores would be closed," I said.

Cathleen clucked her tongue. "Silly Amanda, she's always forgetting something." A typical Cathleen comment, but this time, watching her glow with happiness at her family, I didn't even mind. She may not be perfect, but somewhere along the line, she'd become my friend. I understood that now.

"I'll help Mandy get her bags to her room while you two finish up," Jerry said. He and Mandy went down the hallway together.

"Do you think she knew?" I heard Mandy whisper to her dad.

"Oh, you know your mom, you can never really tell with her." I held in a snicker.

Cathleen came back to the kitchen. She pulled out a carton of eggs and handed them to me. Then we walked together to the front door. "Thanks, Amanda," she said, "for everything. You really came through for me today. You're an amazing woman." She hugged me tightly.

My heart felt so full I thought it would explode.

Cathleen lifted the ends of my hair and pulled back from the hug. "We really do need to do something about these ends, though," she said.

I just hugged her tighter, and then we said our goodbyes.

As I pulled into my own driveway, Ethan and the kids were making a huge snowman. "Come play, Mommy," Becky said, trying to roll a giant ball of snow across the yard.

I nodded. "Let me get my gloves." I went into the house, grabbed my gloves out of the cupboard along with my hat, and headed for the door. As I came through the living room, I saw the nativity and stopped. I pushed the holy family closer together and sighed.

This little scene told the story of more than one small family. Would a nativity be complete without the cows, camels, shepherds, wise men, and angels? I guess it does take a village but not just to raise a child. It takes a village to have a life. It's those people who are there for you—who run to your rescue when you need a reminder of what's important or you feel like you might burn down the house. Cathleen helped Erin, our new friend. Glen helped me, and now it had come around to my turn to help Cathleen. Like it or not, my village contained one of the pushiest women in America and a man who probably lived in a cardboard box.

I love my village for the lessons I learned that Christmas though they came from the most unexpected places.

I said it before; Christmas is all about the gifts. I still believe that's true. What I now realize is that sometimes the most important gifts don't come in packages.

About Ann Acton

Ann Acton lives with her husband and children in a tiny town in Washington State. She loves the feeling of Christmas and usually finishes her shopping on Christmas Eve. She is also the author of *The Miracle Maker*.

To learn more, check out her blog **annacton.com**.

Amy's Star

A Spider Latham
Christmas Story

by

Liz Adair

Amy's Star ~ 1

SPIDER LATHAM GAZED at the green fiberglass box that had just been deposited at the edge of his back patio. A plastic poinsettia wreath hung on the door. "I don't think I've ever seen a porta-potty decorated for Christmas," he said.

"My wife done that." The driver folded up the lift gate. "She said anyone having sewer problems the day before Christmas needed something a little extra."

"Tell her thanks for the thought."

"No problem." The driver took off one work glove and offered his hand. "Bert Cummins."

"Spider Latham." Spider shook his hand.

"Say again?"

"Spider Latham."

"Like?" The driver made his hand look like a spider.

Spider nodded. How many times had he seen people do that? Must be the universal sign for *arachnid*. "It's a nickname." He looked around the back yard. "You ever been up here before?"

"Yeah. I serviced the site when ol' Jack was building this house. We went to school together, Jack Houghton and me."

"Oh?"

"Yeah. I thought he was crazy when he told me he was building a straw bale house. More like a straw bale mansion." Bert pulled his glove back on. "That was really something, him dying so quick like that and leaving everything to you."

The midmorning sun was well above the red cliffs behind his house, and Spider adjusted the brim of his Stetson. "Do you know where the septic tank is?"

Bert, on his way back to his truck, looked around and shrugged. "They put down all these pavers after the bathrooms was in, and it all looks different. He must have a half acre in concrete."

"Well, I'll run down to the courthouse and get the plans. They should be on file."

Bert swung up into the cab. "Don't bank on it. Jack tore down the old home place when he built. I'll bet a dollar he kept the old system. They can tell you down at the courthouse, though."

Spider grimaced. He took two steps back and touched the brim of his hat. "I'd better get a move-on then."

"Yeah. People generally close early on Christmas Eve." Bert shut his door and started his engine.

Spider turned and strode toward his pickup, his three-legged dog, Trey, at his heels. Detouring by the open kitchen window, he tapped on the edge of the screen. Smells of cinnamon and allspice wafted out along with holiday carols from the radio. "I'm going to town," he called. "See if I can get some information on locating the septic tank."

Spider's wife, Laurie, came over to the window, her auburn pony tail bobbing as she leaned over the counter to talk. She wore a red and green apron and had a smudge of flour on her cheek. "I'm sorry this happened just before Christmas. If you can't get it fixed today, we can get by."

"I'll get it taken care of." As Spider headed toward his pickup, he chewed on the last bit of information Bert had given him. No septic plan? Great suffering zot.

Cʒ

Leaving the Planning Department empty handed, Spider almost ran into Toby Flint, a deputy he'd helped on the Red Pueblo problem last August.

"Spider!" Toby's face brightened. "I was just going out to your place."

"Delivering Christmas fruitcake?"

Toby blinked. "No. I hate fruitcake. I wanted to ask a favor."

Spider took a moment to survey the deputy. As always, his pants were creased and the leather on his black duty belt gleamed. "What is it?"

"Well, it's not exactly a favor. It's just that it's Christmas Eve and all."

Spider folded his arms and waited for Toby to get to the point.

Toby's face looked a little less hopeful. "I knew you had taken over Dr. Houghton's wounded birds."

"Wounded birds?"

"Yeah, you know. Amy and the rest of his charity cases."

Spider looked at the deputy searchingly. "You need help, Toby?"

Toby's eyes widened. "What? Me?" He laughed. "No. I'm fine." He looked up and down the hall and then pulled Spider away from the Planning Department door. "It's just that I found this young couple."

Spider frowned as he tried to follow Toby's narrative. "And?"

"He had a pry bar and was hanging around the newspaper stand. Mind you, he hadn't committed any crime."

"No," Spider agreed. "That doesn't sound criminal to me."

"Thing is, they don't have any money, and their car ran out of gas about a mile out of town."

"So, you think they're a couple of wounded birds?"

"They look pretty wounded to me. She looks to be about seventeen, and he's not too much older. They won't say where they're from."

Spider looked at his watch. He was no closer to an answer to his own dilemma, and Toby was trying to complicate his day.

"I gave them some toast," Toby said.

"What do you want me to do?" Impatience put an edge to Spider's voice, and Toby's cheeks began to redden.

"I thought maybe they could stay with you until we were able to locate their family."

"Why don't they stay with you?"

"I'm going up to see my girlfriend. I'm leaving this afternoon."

"What are you doing to locate the family? Are you sure they're as young as you say?"

"I'm tracing the car. As far as being sure, well, no. But wait 'til you see them." Toby was backing away. He must have sensed Spider's softening. "I'll bring them by on my way out of town. You'll see what I mean."

"You haven't yet *said* what you mean." Spider spoke to Toby's back, though. He was already halfway down the hall.

"Huh," Spider grunted, watching the deputy's well-shined heels go out the door.

He immediately dismissed Toby and his wounded birds and returned to the problem at hand. Next stop had to be Ace Hardware.

Amy's Star ~ 2

ENTERING THE HARDWARE store, Spider set a course for the plumbing department. A clerk, name tag of Hank, met him at a stack of black pipe. "Anything I can do for you?"

"I'm looking for a probe. I've got to find a septic tank."

"How deep is it buried?"

"I haven't a clue."

"Where's it located?"

"It's Jack Houghton's place. You familiar with it?"

Hank shook his head. "Don't know that I am. We don't have any probes here at the store, but I've got one at home I'll loan you."

Spider looked at his watch. How long would he have to cool his heels waiting for Hank to get off?

Hank fished a set of keys out of his pocket. "My truck is out back. C'mon, and we'll run over and get it. Won't take but a minute."

Spider followed him out through the back door and over to a yellow '83 Chevy pickup. Hank got in and leaned over to unlock the passenger door.

Spider climbed in and smelled the familiar old-pickup smell of oil and dust. "I appreciate your doing this."

"Glad to do it." Hank started the engine, jockeyed around a forklift with a load of bricks, and pulled onto a city street heading north. "In fact, it's lucky for me."

"Oh?" Spider shifted in his seat. "How's that?"

"Well, I know you inherited Dr. Houghton's place."

"Yeah?"

"And along with that, you inherited Amy."

"Yeah. That too."

"Well..." Hank pulled into a driveway and braked to a stop, but he didn't finish his thought.

"You were saying," Spider prompted.

Hank cleared his throat. "Well, it may be nothing."

"But?"

"But she came in this morning and bought me out of Christmas lights."

"Christmas lights? When was this?"

"About a half hour before you came in."

Spider rubbed his jaw. "I wonder why she did that."

"She said something about the Bethlehem star." Hank left the motor running and opened his door. "Let me go get that probe, and I'll tell you about the rest of it on the way back."

Hank punched a button on the visor, got out, and ducked under the slowly rising garage door. Moments later he reappeared carrying a steel rod with a T-handle on top that he tossed in the bed, and then he got in the truck.

Spider watched him press the button to lower the door. "What's this about the Bethlehem star?"

Hank looked over his shoulder as he backed out. "I don't know. But she was grinning from ear to ear and told me she had been called to recreate the star right here in Kanab."

Spider's brows drew together. "She said *called*? Like it was a church assignment?"

Hank took off his baseball cap and put it on the dash. He hunched a shoulder and glanced at Spider. "I don't like saying this, but I thought you ought to know."

"Saying what? Know what? You haven't told me much yet."

"Well, the thing is, I know Amy's being treated for...that she's—"

"Bipolar," Spider said. Why did he feel so defensive? Amy wasn't his child. He hadn't even known her before last August.

"Yeah," Hank said. "The thing is, I remember how Amy was the day before she tried to ride in the Western Legends parade as Lady Godiva. She came into the store and bought a grundle of flat washers and some gold paint. She was fixin' to wire them together and make a kind of chain mail for her horse—it turned out great, by the way."

"If anyone had looked at it. I imagine all eyes were on her."

The corners of Hank's lips lifted. "Yep. She was quite a sight."

It irked Spider that the smile lingered for a full city block. "You were saying you remember how she was when she came in to get the washers."

"Oh. Right. Well, like I was saying, when she came in to get the washers, she was like she was this morning. Big grin. Spilling over with information about what she was going to do. Talking a mile a minute. If you don't mind my saying so, she seemed a bit manic."

Spider sighed. "I suppose everyone in town knows about her illness."

Hank seemed to think it over and then nodded. "You know that saying—it takes a village to raise a child? Well, it takes a village to watch out for Amy, too."

"Sounds more like the village was staring at her."

Hank shook his head decisively. "I was at the staging area for the parade, and as soon as she rode up, somebody grabbed the raffle quilt and wrapped it around her."

"Did she ride in the parade?"

"Nah. Someone called Dr. Houghton, and he came and got her." Hank turned into the lumberyard and parked his pickup. "But today was like that. Made me wonder if she might need to see her doctor."

Spider's jaw tightened. It seemed like everyone was a diagnostician. "I'll check it out, but tell me again what she said about the star."

Hank turned off the key and grabbed his hat off the dash. "I told you all I know. She said she had been called to recreate the Bethlehem star."

"Here in Kanab?"

"Yes. Here in Kanab." Hank got out and closed the door.

Spider got out, too, and stood on the other side of the pickup bed. "Did she say *who* had called her?"

Hank, hat still in his hand, scratched his head and then raised his eyes to meet Spider's. "Holy cow."

"What do you mean, holy cow?"

"I thought she was talking about something else."

Spider reached in and got the probe, hefting it like he would a spear. "Spit it out, man. Tell me what she said."

Hank took the time to put on his hat. His eyes went from the long metal rod in Spider's hand to his face and back. "She said it was President Obama."

Spider spoke under his breath. "Great suffering zot." He took off for the parking lot, pausing to look back at Hank and lift the tool. "Thanks for this. I'll bring it back after Christmas."

"No problem."

Spider strode to his pickup and dropped the probe in the back. As he got in, he pulled his cell phone out of his pocket and brought up Laurie's number.

Christmas music in the background told him she had answered before he heard her greeting.

"Hello, Darlin'," he said. "Has Amy come home yet?"

"No. I haven't seen her. She called a while ago from Crosby's Hardware asking how long your heavy duty extension cord was."

"Not Ace Hardware?"

"No. I'm sure she said Crosby's. Why?"

"I think we've got a problem. This one may be bigger than the drains."

Amy's Star ~ 3

WHEN SPIDER GOT home, he saw that Amy's pickup was in the driveway with cardboard boxes stacked high above the sides of the bed. Trey came to meet him, and he leaned down to pat her head. "Where's Amy, Trey dog? Let's see if she's in the kitchen."

At the back door, he could see Laurie at the table with Amy opposite. They both looked up as Spider opened the door.

"Hi," Laurie said. She smiled, but it wasn't an automatic, come-from-the-heart, Christmas Eve smile. It was a wooden, brave-faced turning up of her lips.

Amy smiled, too. Hers was genuine. Five-hundred-watt incandescent.

"Hello, girls," Spider said. "How's it going?"

"Fantastic," Amy said. "Did you see the back of my truck?"

"Caught a glimpse of it." He turned one of the chairs around and straddled it, putting his Stetson on the table. "Is that my Christmas present?"

Amy laughed. "Your present has been under the tree for a week. I know you know because I saw you shaking it the other day."

Laurie broke in. "Amy stopped taking her meds."

"So I heard." Spider tipped his head, regarding Amy. "Is that wise?"

Amy covered her face. "No. I know it's not, but listen." She let her hands slide down, so her eyes were peeking above her fingertips. "I just wanted to feel the Christmas joy. You don't know what it's like to have everything—" She made a horizontal motion. "—even out. I want to *feel something* this Christmas!"

Spider grimaced. He understood what Amy was saying, and right now he hated the responsibility he had inherited. "This thing with President Obama and the Bethlehem star. It wasn't real, you know."

Amy stared at Spider, chewing on her lower lip. "The big black limo? The tinted windows going silently down?" She pantomimed the windows lowering. "The man in the back leaning forward and taking my hand, telling me he had this great thing for me to do? You're saying it wasn't real?"

Spider nodded. "That's what I'm saying."

Amy looked at Laurie. "It was real to me."

The stove buzzer sounded, and Laurie jumped up and grabbed a hot pad. As she opened the oven, she spoke over her shoulder. "What about after Christmas? What then?"

Amy raised her hand like she was testifying. "Day after tomorrow. Back on my meds. I promise."

Spider pointed. "That's your left hand."

Amy's grin grew in size. "That means the promise goes double."

Spider stood. "It better."

Amy stood, too. "Besides, I've got so much to do before tonight, I need all this energy."

Spider put the chair back and picked up his hat. "Bethlehem star, huh?"

"It's gonna be spectacular!" Amy hugged Laurie, catching her with a cookie mid-way from the pan to the cooling rack. "Oops. Five second rule. I'll eat that one." She bent down to pick up the snickerdoodle that had fallen to the floor.

Spider set his Stetson on his head, still speaking to Amy. "Did Laurie tell you about the drain situation?"

Amy nodded and answered with her mouth full. "Go potty in the privy outside. Shower standing in a washtub. All water gets thrown on the flowerbeds. I got it."

Spider picked up one of the cool cookies and regarded Amy. She was short and square, and her straight blonde hair hung in a pixie cut over her blue eyes.

"How long did you live here with Jack?" he asked. "Do you know where the septic tank is?"

Amy shook her head. "I'd help you look, but I've got to find a place to put my star. Want to help me for a minute?"

Spider looked at his watch. The morning was just

about gone. In a couple hours, any parts he might need to fix the drains would be out of reach as stores closed for Christmas.

"Spider?" Laurie came over to him and spoke softly. "It's Christmas. This one needs to last her a lifetime."

"Unless she makes the holiday med vacation an annual affair," he murmured. "But okay." He held up his hands. "If you don't mind freezing your buns off tonight going out to the privy, I'm fine with that."

Laurie grinned. "I'll warm them up on you when I come back in."

Spider pulled her to him. "I'm fine with that, too." He planted a kiss on her mouth.

Amy spoke from the back door. "Pul-eeze. You've got a tender young thing listening to this. I'm blushing."

Spider snorted, but he refrained from any comments about Lady Godiva as he followed Amy out.

Spider left his jacket on the peg by the door. It was a shirtsleeve-weather day, and the sun took any edge off the preceding night's December chill as it climbed toward noon. "What do you need me to do?" he asked as they crossed the expanse of pavers.

She stopped at the edge and pointed to the red bluff that began rising about a hundred yards in back of the barn. "See the tree at the top?"

"You planning on putting your star on top of that tree?"

Amy shook her head. "I want to anchor one end of a line on that tree and the other end down here somewhere. I need you to help me do that."

"You're going to have a heck of a lot of line," Spider said. "Stores close in a couple of hours."

"I got a thousand feet of poly rope. That's all Crosby's had."

"That'll do." Spider traced the trajectory from the cliff down to the base of the barn. "Let's go have a look-see, figure what we can hook onto."

They found an eyebolt in the barn foundation, and fifteen minutes later, Amy was jogging up a trail with a ball of parachute cord in her hand.

"Call me when you get to the top," Spider shouted after her.

She waved to show she heard him and continued her ascent.

He stood watching for a moment and then went to his pickup to get the probe. Returning to the back yard with Trey at his heels, he surveyed the area. The pavers were laid out in a random pattern that created an attractive, low maintenance, low water landscape. But where was the septic access?

He crossed to the open kitchen window and tapped on the frame. "Laurie, can you come out for a minute?"

The back door opened. "What d'ya need?" she asked.

"You came to visit Jack when he was young. Do you know where the old house was located?"

She stepped out onto the patio and walked from the covered area into the sunshine. Shading her eyes, she looked around. "Everything's different, but I think the old home place was in this same spot. I think Jack tore it down and built his house in the same place."

"Huh."

"What's that?"

"I just said huh."

"No. It sounds like a truck coming up the driveway." Laurie walked over to look through the breezeway between the house and the garage. "It's a tow truck," she called back to Spider. "And Toby's right behind."

"Aw, shoot. Toby's wounded birds." Spider strode over to Laurie and stood, hands on hips, as Deputy Flint got out of his pickup.

"Toby's bringing us some birds?"

Spider didn't answer Laurie but called to the deputy, "I thought you were coming after lunch."

"I was, but I need to get up the road. I figured a couple hours sooner wasn't going to change anything drastically." Toby beckoned. "Come and meet Grace and Ben."

Spider waved to Vic, the tow truck driver who had gotten out and was busy unloading a tired looking Honda Civic. When Spider turned back to greet his Christmas guests, he silently agreed with Toby's assessment. Neither one looked over seventeen.

The young man was of average height but thin

and pale. The girl, waif-like, had dark eyes too big for her face. She pulled her shapeless cardigan around her, but it couldn't disguise the size and shape of her belly. It looked like she was hiding a basketball under her tee shirt.

Spider's heart sank. A wounded bird for sure—one that looked like it was about ready to lay an egg.

Amy's Star ~ 4

LAURIE SWEPT BY Spider and put an arm around each of the young people. "We're so glad to have you," she said. "Are you staying for Christmas? That will be nice."

Neither of the visitors said a word, but as they walked through the breezeway with Laurie, the waif bent down to rub Trey behind the ears.

Spider turned to Toby. "What have you found out? Who are they?"

"I know their first names. Grace and Ben."

"You said that. What else? Didn't he have a driver's license? Car registration?"

Toby turned up his hands. "What do you want me to say? They wouldn't tell me who they are."

"You're tracing the car?"

"Yeah, but it's Christmas Eve." Toby looked at his watch. "I gotta get going." He patted his pocket. "It's gonna be a special Christmas in Panguitch."

"Oh?"

Toby waved at the departing tow truck. "Yes, sir. I'm gonna pop the old question-a-roonie."

Spider smiled. "Is that right? Well, you'd better get on the road."

Toby twisted his hands together. "You got any words of advice, Spider?"

"Me? Why would you want advice from me?"

"Well, you know. You and Laurie. You've got a good thing going. How'd you ask her?"

Spider laughed. "She asked me. I was beating around the bush, making a hash of it. Ring in my pocket, just like you. Finally she said, 'You want to get married?' I said yep, and there you go."

Toby kicked a rock off the driveway. "I don't know if that makes me feel better or not."

"Nothing will make you feel better until you give it a go. Now, on your way. I'll take care of those two young 'uns until you find out where they belong."

"You're right. I've just got to do it." Toby sketched a salute and turned to his pickup. As he got in the cab, he called, "Merry Christmas."

"Merry Christmas. Call me as soon as you know anything." Spider waved and turned to walk back through the breezeway to the back yard. He paused there, wanting to get started on finding the septic tank but knowing he should go in and make conversation with their guests.

He looked up at the cliff with its red rocks sharply outlined against the cobalt sky and searched for Amy. There she was halfway up. He'd pop into the house for a minute. Amy's shout would be a good excuse to leave.

As he opened the back door, he breathed in the heavy fragrance of onions and celery floating on vaporized molecules of chicken fat. Spying Grace and Ben single-mindedly consuming bowls of soup, Spider asked, "Is it lunchtime already?"

"Not yet. They haven't had a meal since yesterday morning, so I gave them some soup to hold them over until noon. I intended to make rolls, but today hasn't turned out the way I planned."

Grace paused with her spoon halfway to her mouth and turned her dark, sad eyes on Laurie.

"Oh, not you dear." Laurie moved over to squeeze her shoulders. "I meant the drain thing."

Ben showed the most life since they had pulled in. He sat up and looked from Laurie to Spider and back. "What about the drains?"

Spider answered. "They're plugged."

"Did you try a snake?"

Spider gritted his teeth, counted to five, and tried to remove the edge from his reply. "Yeah."

Ben finished his soup in three hasty bites and stood. "Where's your septic tank?"

Laurie must have seen that Spider didn't have the patience to answer questions from someone who looked like he hadn't yet begun shaving. She answered. "We're not sure where it is."

Spider opened the door. "I'm going out to see if I can find it."

"I'll come help," Ben said. "You got a probe?"

Without answering, Spider went out, walked to the middle of the patio, and looked up at the bluff behind the barn. He could see Amy, a toy soldier in a white blouse, scrambling to the top.

"What're you looking at?" Ben asked.

Spider pointed. "Amy. She just made it to the top. C'mon."

Ben walked beside Spider as he strode to the barn. "We're going up there?"

"Nah. She's going to throw a line down and pull up a rope."

"What for?"

"She's going to hang a Bethlehem star as high as she can. She's going to hook the rope to that tree that sits on the edge."

"Cool."

Spider walked to the back of the barn where a crowbar leaned against the wall. Amy's spool of poly rope sat by it.

"So, how's she planning on getting her star up there?" Ben asked, still tagging along.

"I haven't asked her."

"If you put a loop in the rope out about fifty feet, that'd give you enough to go around the tree and go over the bank. If you had a pulley, you could hang it on that loop, and you'd have an easy way to get the star up." Ben looked up at the tree again. "How high you figure that is?"

"Probably three hundred feet. Maybe more."

"You got a pulley?"

Spider regarded the young man. He didn't look like much. His face was thin, and his eyes were a washed-out blue with light-colored eyelashes, but he had shed his jacket in the mildness of the day, and his arms looked like he was used to physical work. "You know how to tie a bowline?" Spider asked.

"Sure."

"I'm not sure Amy does. Do you want to hike up there and help, if she needs it? Don't let her tie a granny."

Ben glanced around. "Where's the trail?"

Spider pointed. "Behind the garden plot. It snakes up from there."

Ben nodded and started off at a trot.

"Good idea about the pulley," Spider called after him.

He raised a hand in acknowledgement as he continued up the trail.

Spider went to his newly built shop on the other side of the barn. He and Laurie had gone round and round about what the shop would look like. Spider had said they couldn't afford anything but a metal clad pole building, but Laurie was adamant that the shop should match the Pueblo-type architecture of house and barn.

"We've got the money. We can afford it," she had said.

"It's Jack's money," Spider had countered.

"It's yours now. The shop matches."

She got the last word, and Spider had to admit she'd been right. He entered the shop and quickly found the pulley he needed. He grabbed another large coil of parachute cord and stuffed it under his arm. Standing a moment beside the workbench, he mentally walked through the process of hooking the rope to the eyebolt. He decided he needed a come-along to cinch it tight and lifted one down from the pegboard wall. Then he returned to the area behind the barn where they were going to tether the star.

He pulled out fifty feet of Amy's rope and, heeding Ben's suggestion, tied a loop and attached the pulley. He had just finished when his phone rang. He searched three pockets before he found it. "Yeah?"

Amy was on the other end. "Ben tossed down the line. We're ready to haul up the rope."

"Okay. Give me a minute to get to the bottom of the cliff."

"We can see you."

Spider looked up, and when Amy waved he waved the pulley in reply. "Anything else?"

"Just that I can tie a bowline. But thanks for sending Ben up. He's got a better arm than I do for hucking the line down."

"No problem." Spider punched the off button then grabbed the pry bar leaning against the barn and put it through the hole in the rope reel. He hung the bundle of parachute cord on it, too, and picked up the pulley.

It was an awkward load, but he managed to call Laurie while he walked towards the bluff. When she answered, he asked her to come out and help for a minute.

By the time he reached the red, rocky scree at the bottom of the bluff, Laurie had trotted out to join him. Grace followed at a more sedate pace with the dog beside her.

"It's a ways out here," Laurie said, puffing a bit. "What d'ya need?"

Spider had dropped his burdens and had his hands on his hips, scanning the area. "We need to find the line Amy and Ben threw down from the top."

Laurie's auburn pony tail hung halfway down her back as she shaded her eyes and craned her neck. "Are they up there?"

"Yeah. They're back from the edge, though. You won't be able to see them."

Grace joined them. "Is that what you're looking for?"

Spider searched the area she was pointing to and finally saw the white cord hanging down. "That's it," he called. He strode to where the cord lay on the ground. He had tied a heavy bolt on the end for ballast, and he removed that now, dropped it in his pocket, and tied the cord through a loop he had put in the end of the poly rope.

"What do you need me to do?" Laurie asked.

"You see the pulley?" Spider tossed the bundle of cord to her.

She picked up the parachute line. "Wow. Do you think you have enough of this?"

"It's got to reach to the top and back down," Spider said. "I need you to thread it through the pulley and let it unwind. Keep track of both ends as Amy pulls the rope up."

"I can help you," Grace said. "You hold the pulley, and I'll put the cord through."

Spider started walking toward the barn. "I'm going to unroll the rope and get ready to tie it off to the barn as soon as she gets it up there." The reel spun on the pry-bar axle leaving a line of rope in the dirt. When he got halfway there, Amy called on her phone.

"Can I start hauling up?"

Spider glanced at Laurie and Grace. They looked ready. "Haul away," he said. "When you get it tied off to the tree, come on down and we'll have lunch."

It took them almost an hour to get the rope up and anchored from the tree to the barn. The pulley hung about ten feet below the top of the bluff, the double length of parachute cord trailing to the bottom. They were ready to hoist up the Bethlehem star.

Amy shouted down from the top. "Wow-ee! It's gonna be spectacular!"

Amy's Star ~ 5

SPIDER BLEW ON his spoonful of soup to cool it. "So," he said in a conversational tone. "We haven't had a chance to get through the usual small talk with Ben and Grace. Might as well do that right now."

"Oh, I don't know," Laurie said, her eyes twinkling. "Grace and I did some small talking."

Grace looked down at her soup. "Very small, I'm afraid."

Laurie patted her hand. "Don't worry, dear. We don't need a lot of information. We're just glad you're with us for Christmas."

Amy looked around the table. "What's going on?"

Laurie smiled. "Grace and Ben were on their way south, but they ran out of gas. Their resources are slender at the moment."

"Jack used to call it embarrassed circumstances." Amy chuckled. "He brought so many people home in that condition that we started shortening it to EC." Leaning her chin on her fist, she asked Grace, "Where were you going?"

Ben's and Grace's eyes met, and he answered the question. "We'd rather not say."

Amy shrugged. "Suit yourself." She turned to Laurie. "How's Goldie doing?"

Laurie grimaced. "I think she's getting close. I checked her this morning, and all the signs point to tomorrow or the next day." She turned to Ben and Grace to explain. "We're keeping a horse for a friend who is away for several years."

"She's in the slammer," Amy added.

Laurie put her hand on Amy's knee and went on with her explanation. "I didn't realize that the mare was pregnant, but when I talked to Dorrie, the owner, she said that last winter a wild stallion jumped the fence and was in Goldie's pasture. Dorrie didn't know she had been bred."

"And she wasn't supposed to let her have any babies," Spider said. "Goldie has a deformed hoof that's hereditary. She could pass it on to her foal."

Grace looked at Spider with her large, waif eyes. "That's terrible."

"Well, it's done now. We'll just see what happens." Laurie pushed the soup pot toward her guests. "Have some more."

Grace put up her hands. "I couldn't eat another bite. Thank you. It was so good."

"Both times," Ben said.

Laurie stood and began gathering dishes. "Well, save room for dinner. We'll have turkey and trimmings tonight and leftovers tomorrow."

Grace stood too, her hand on her back. "Can I help you with dinner?"

"Sure." Laurie's brows came together as she looked up from the pile of crockery. "Is something wrong?"

Grace rubbed a spot in her lumbar area. "I've got this pain that comes and goes. Must be from sleeping in the car last night."

Spider stood and pushed his chair in. "Well, you'll sleep well tonight. The east guest room has a king sized bed in it."

Neither Ben nor Grace said anything but both had a rosy flush climb up their cheeks. She looked at her feet. He looked at the back door as if seeking an escape route.

Ben slowly stood. "Um. We're not..." He pointed from himself to Grace. "We're not married or anything like that."

In the silence that followed Ben's remark, Spider studiously avoided looking at Grace's pregnant belly. Laurie resumed stacking soup bowls, and Spider joined her, glad for something to occupy his attention.

Amy was the one who finally spoke. "Who's going to help me with the Bethlehem star?"

Ben and Grace spoke together. "I will."

Grace looked at Laurie. "Unless you need me right now to help with dinner."

"No," Laurie said. "You go on. If you'll come in about four, that'll be plenty of time."

Spider paused on his way to the sink with his hands full of dishes. "I'd better see if I can find the septic tank, Amy. Call me if you need me, though."

"I will," she promised. Then she clattered out the door with Grace right behind her.

The last in line, Ben paused with his hand on the knob. "Oh, by the way. I've got an idea where the tank might be."

"Oh?" Spider wiped his hands on a dishtowel.

Ben held the door open. "Come and see."

Spider took his hat off the hook by the door and followed Ben outside.

Pointing to where pavers were laid in a pinwheel pattern, Ben said, "I think this may be where it is. See, the pattern for the pavers all over the back yard starts here."

"Huh," Spider grunted. "You may be right."

"I saw it from up above. From down here it all looks pretty random."

Spider's eyes traced the lines as they spiraled out from the few tiles under his feet. Funny he had never noticed the pattern that spread out from here, halfway between the back door and the breezeway. Thirty feet away from the house, it wasn't a high traffic area.

"Only one way to find out if it's under here," Spider said. "They're sand-set pavers. They'll come up easy."

"Want help?"

Spider's attention was captured by the laughter of Amy and Grace coming through the breezeway, each on an end of a roll of chicken wire with Trey following close behind. "Should Grace be carrying that? Maybe you'd better go help them."

"Omygosh!" Ben took off at a trot, calling, "Grace, let me take that for you."

Spider paused to watch him take the wire roll, hoist it on his shoulder, and follow Amy toward the back of the barn. Grace brought up the rear, resting at the corner of the barn, leaning her shoulder against the wall with her hand on the small of her back. Better keep an eye on that.

Then he headed through the breezeway to get the tools he needed to test out Ben's theory about what lay under the paver pinwheel.

Amy's Star ~ 6

WHILE THE YOUNG folks worked on Amy's star, Spider found the septic tank, right where Ben thought it would be. He called Burt Cummins and made arrangements for him to come and pump it out first thing the day after Christmas.

Satisfied with that small accomplishment, he put his tools away and came into the shop to finish Laurie's Christmas present. He had made a branding iron for her with her *Double L* brand and still needed to paint the wooden handle.

He took a small can of enamel off a shelf and began to shake it. Laurie liked red. Still shaking with the can with one hand, he chose a paintbrush and set it on the bench. The door opened behind him, and he sprang in front of the bench, spreading his arms to conceal the gift.

Ben peeked through the door. "Okay if I come in?"

Spider exhaled. "You scared me."

Ben remained with just his shoulder in the door.

"Come on in," Spider invited. "I'm finishing up something I made for Laurie."

Ben approached the workbench. "That's an interesting Christmas present."

"She's been wanting one." Spider brushed a wood shaving off the bench. "By the way, I didn't tell you thanks for pointing me in the right direction to find that tank."

"Glad to help." Ben put his hands in his pockets and looked around. "This is quite a shop."

"It's a work in progress." Spider leaned against the workbench. "Everything going all right in the Bethlehem star department?"

Ben folded his arms and rested his weight on the bench, too. "That Amy is a gal with a plan. Did you know she bought ten thousand lights?"

"Ten thousand!"

Ben smiled. "I talked her out of using all of them. They're LED, so they don't draw what regular lights do, but I don't think she realized that she can't string out that much extension cord without losing significant power."

"Oh, shoot!" Spider grimaced. "I've been so uptight about the drain situation that I didn't even think of that."

Ben stood and looked around again. "You got a generator?"

"Yeah. What're you thinking?"

"I figured if we put it right below the star, then we'd only have to run cord from the generator up to where it's hanging. We could manage that."

"The generator's in the storeroom. Let's go get it."

Spider led the way through a wide door into a room full of large tools and equipment laid out on industrial shelving. The generator sat underneath the shelves on the floor, and Spider pointed to it.

Ben pulled it out and stood up, hands on hips. "Grace's pregnant," he said.

"Beg pardon?"

Ben ran his hand through his hair. "You took us in. Fed us. I don't feel good about keeping things secret, even though Grace wants me to."

Spider stifled a smile. "I hate to tell you this, Ben, but Grace being pregnant is no secret."

Ben made an impatient gesture. "I know that, but I meant the story behind it all."

Spider pulled a stack of empty five gallon buckets from the shelf beside him. He pulled off two, handing one to Ben and turning the other over on the concrete floor. "Have a seat, son, and tell me your story. Start from the beginning."

Ben sat on his makeshift stool and leaned back, propping himself against the shelving brace. "The beginning." He screwed up his face in thought. "I would say the beginning was my junior year in high school."

"Where was that?"

"Salt Lake City. I had been placed with a new foster family, and that meant a new school. Grace and I had fifth period choir together."

"You're smiling," Spider observed. "Must be a nice memory."

"It is. I fell in love with her on that first day."

"And she? Did she reciprocate?"

"It took a year to win her, but by Christmas of our senior year—last Christmas—she told me she loved me." Ben sighed. "But..."

"Let me guess," Spider said. "Her family didn't want her getting serious so early."

"There's just her and her mom. But I think it was more than her getting serious so young."

"What was it, then?"

Ben shrugged. "I didn't have the proper background. Or aspirations."

Spider's brows went up. "How so?"

"Well, first there was the foster child thing. Maybe that would have been overlooked if I had earned a scholarship to a prestigious school."

"No scholarship, huh?"

Ben smiled and looked down at his shoes. "Oh I got a scholarship."

"Must have been to a state college."

Ben shook his head. "Worse. It was to a tech school in Phoenix that was coupled with an electrician apprenticeship." He looked up at Spider, his eyes sparkling. "It's a great program. I can support myself while I go to school. And when I finish, I'll have a good paying job."

"And you have a natural aptitude."

Ben paused, as if struck by what Spider had said. "You know, I do have an aptitude. I'm top of my class."

Spider folded his arms and stretched his long legs out in front of him. "But, Grace's mama wasn't going to have her tying herself to someone who worked with his hands."

Ben's brows came down, and his mouth formed a grim line. "You got that right. When spring break rolled around, Mrs. Engle set Grace up with the son of her boss. He was a college man. Princeton."

"I suppose he had the right background and aspirations."

Ben picked up a bolt lying on the shelf beside him and began unscrewing the nut from the end, his eyes on the task. "He might have had the right aspirations, but he had no morals and nothing against drugging and raping a young girl."

"Great suffering zot! Is that what happened?"

Ben nodded, still intent on the piece of metal in his hands.

"What did Grace's mother say?"

"Grace never told her."

Spider whistled under his breath. "So the mother doesn't know? How could that happen?"

Ben finally looked up. "Grace's mother is a career woman, a producer for a TV station in Salt Lake. Very successful. Very busy. She loves Grace, but her way of showing it always has to do with things that will bring prestige."

"Like getting her a date with a Princeton man?"

Ben nodded. "Or sending her to an expensive school."

"Where is this school?"

"It's a performing arts college in Seattle. Grace left Salt Lake in mid-August."

"And she didn't come home for Thanksgiving?"

When Ben shook his head in reply, Spider counted on his fingers. "So she'd have been five months along when she left?"

"About four and a half, the best I can figure." Ben's cheeks got red. "I don't know much about it, but I've done some reading online since she told me."

"And she told you when?"

"What's today? Wednesday? She called me Saturday. Her mother had sent her the plane tickets home, and she didn't know what to do. I was the first one she'd told."

"This last Saturday?" Spider pulled his legs in and sat forward, frowning. "Great suffering zot! Did she think if she ignored the situation it would go away?"

Ben laid the bolt back on the shelf beside him and looked Spider in the eye. "I won't let you be angry with her. She's gone through a hellish four months in a strange place with no friends and no one to help her." Ben dropped his eyes. "I should have been there for her, but when she quit emailing or calling, I figured it was because she had finally listened to her mother."

Spider patted Ben's knee. "I'm not angry with her, son, but why'd she quit writing?"

"She thought—" Ben's voice broke, and he had to try again. "She thought I wouldn't love her anymore because of what happened." He paused and cleared his throat. "Anyway, she called me, and I said I'd pick her up and take her home with me. She changed her tickets, but because of the holiday, the nearest flight she could find was to Las Vegas." He spread his hands. "I had enough money for gas both ways, but then my starter went out."

"And there went your gas money," Spider said. "I understand. But, if you were going to Phoenix, why come this way? It's closer from Las Vegas to go by Kingman."

"One of my instructors got me a day's work at the trading post at Cameron. My plan was to work there today, and we could be home by Christmas."

"So what're you going to do when you get to Phoenix?"

"Get married. I've got a small apartment. It's a studio, but there'll be room for the baby, too. We'll manage."

Spider rubbed his jaw. "That sounds okay, but what about her mother? If Grace didn't arrive at the airport on her scheduled flight, wouldn't her mom do something? Like call out the police?"

Ben shook his head. "Her flight was scheduled for today, and Mrs. Engle is working tonight. She does it every year, so more of the crew can be off. Grace was supposed to take a cab home and see her mom in the morning."

Spider stood and picked up his bucket. "Okay. But if you're going to marry Grace, you need to start off right. Be square with her mom. If Grace won't call her mother, you need to do it. Let her know her daughter is safe and that you intend to take care of her—and the baby—from now on."

Ben smacked his palm down on one of the steel shelves and spoke through clenched teeth. "I just know she's going to think I did this to Grace."

"She may at first, but that's not important. What's important is your relationship with Grace. Mrs. Engle will soon see that her daughter made the right choice."

Ben rose and gave Spider his bucket. "You're right. If I'm at odds with her mom, Grace'll suffer."

Spider put the stack back on the shelf and looked at his watch. "You'd better get that generator out there and get it hooked up before dark. Put it in the back of the old pickup to get it out there, the one with the dented roof." He pulled a key ring from his pocket, showed Ben the right key, and handed them to him. "Just leave the truck there for tonight."

Ben pocketed the keys and rolled the generator to the storeroom door. He got it over the threshold and halfway to the shop entrance before he stopped. "You should see the star that Amy designed," he said. "Want to come help?"

Spider went to his workbench and picked up the can of red paint. "I need to get this done. You go on."

"Okay." Ben opened the shop door. "But wait 'til you see it. It's going to be spectacular."

Amy's Star ~ 7

DINNER WAS A merry affair. The turkey, brown and succulent, looked like something out of a magazine. Ben declared Grace's mashed potatoes and Amy's bread stuffing amazing, and everyone agreed. They topped it off with pumpkin pie, and then all worked together to put the food away and get the dishes done. Amy washed them in a dishpan and carried the water outside after they were done and dumped it on the chrysanthemums.

"We're eating reruns tomorrow," Laurie announced.

"Suits me." Ben put a stack of plastic storage containers in the fridge.

Laurie paused with a dishcloth in her hand, looked at the clock, and then at Spider. "I think I need to go out to the stable. Can we do our Christmas Eve out there?"

"You think Goldie's that close?"

Grace's eyes grew huge. "Are you frightened?"

Laurie smiled at her. "No. I'm sure she can handle everything herself. Being there is more for me than for the mare."

"I'll put the Buddy heater in the tack room and grab two cots," Spider said.

"You're keeping me company?" Laurie kissed him on the cheek. "We'll need camp chairs, too." She finished wiping the counters and set the cloth by the sink. "Better get your jackets," she said to Amy and Grace. "And grab some blankets from the upstairs hall closet."

"I'll get them," Amy said, trotting through the living room to the broad staircase that swept up to the second floor. She stopped halfway and leaned against the wrought iron railing. "Spider, when we read the Christmas story, we need to have the star shining above us," she called. "It's dark out. Let's turn it on right now."

Spider laughed as he put on his Stetson. "Okay. As soon as we get everything out to the tack room, we'll all go out and watch as you plug it in."

Everyone helped carry blankets, and they trooped out through the back door.

"Brrr. It's chilly," Laurie said.

"Not bad for December," Spider said. "It's supposed to stay above freezing tonight."

"Are you rethinking whether you want to spend the night in the barn?" Amy asked.

"We'll be fine. The heater will keep it warm." Spider opened the tack room door, held it for everyone to enter, and followed the group inside. He dropped the quilts on a saddle rack and spoke to Ben. "Want to help me get the rest of the gear?"

Ben set his blankets on an adjacent rack and followed Spider outside. "Boy it's dark!" he said as Spider closed the door behind them.

"Not much of a moon." Spider pulled a flashlight out of his jacket pocket. "We'll have a crescent later, but it's not up yet."

Ben put his hands in his pocket and paused to look up at the black matte sky studded with twinkling points of light. "Amy's star should show up pretty good."

They reached the shop, and Spider opened the door and turned on the light. Back in the storeroom, they found everything they needed and retraced their way to the shop door. Spider let Ben go first then balanced his load, so he could reach the switch.

Before he could flip it down, the lights went out.

"Whoa!" Ben said. "Did you do that?"

"Do what?"

"Turn out all the lights?" Ben walked a few tentative steps. "Oh, wow."

"What?"

"Look toward Kanab. The whole countryside is dark."

"Huh." Spider juggled his burdens, so he could

close the door and then get the flashlight out of his pocket. "Wonder what happened." He turned on the torch and they followed the circle of light to the stable and opened the door.

Laurie's voice sounded loud in the dark. "Spider? Did you flip a breaker?"

"Nope. The power's off all over."

"What do you mean by all over?" Grace's voice trembled, and Spider found her with the beam. Careful not to shine it in her face, he kept her illuminated until Ben could set the heater down and go to her.

Spider lowered the chairs and cots to the floor. "Amy, I'm going to ask you to wait a while longer for your star. I'll go get some more flashlights and a couple of lanterns. Hang tough. You won't be in the dark much longer."

As he stepped out the door, he heard an intake of breath and then Grace's tremulous voice. "Is he taking the light?"

"I'll be right back," Spider promised and set off toward the shop again.

Finding what he needed proved more difficult than he would have thought. With only the flashlight's slender beam to aid him, he finally found the lanterns hanging on the pegboard. He located spare batteries and the place on a high shelf where he had stashed four extra flashlights. With his arms full, he pulled the door closed and walked as quickly as he could to the stable.

When he opened the tack room door, he was greeted by Amy's cheer. "Now it's starlight time."

"Wait a minute," Spider said. "Everyone gets a flashlight."

Someone exhaled, and then Grace spoke, her voice stouter now. "Thank you."

Spider handed out lights, and when all were ready, he announced, "It is now time to turn on Amy's Bethlehem star."

Out of the tack room, they went around to the back of the barn and tramped across the field. Spider oriented himself by illuminated glimpses of the pickup that held the generator, sitting three hundred feet below Amy's chicken wire contraption. He looked up but could see nothing except the dark outline of the cliff blocking out the view of the spangled sky.

Spider heard somebody stumble and shined his light to see who it was. "Careful, Grace," he said.

"I've got her," Ben answered. "You guys go on. We're going to stop and rest a moment."

Spider paused, trying to see from Grace's countenance how she was doing. Her hand was on her back, and her mouth was compressed, but she looked toward Spider and smiled. "I'm fine," she said. "Just a stitch in my back."

"Okay," Spider said. "But call if it doesn't get better."

"It's better already," Grace said.

Spider turned his flashlight back to the ground in front of him and continued the trek to the pickup.

Laurie, walking beside him, said in a low voice, "I don't like the look of that back ache."

"You think Goldie isn't the only one that's getting close to time?" Spider looked back and saw the twin beams of Ben and Grace's flashlights bobbing as they walked. "If that's so, is it all right for her to be way out here in the dark?"

"She'll be fine. The walk is probably good for her." Laurie glanced around and then added, "It would probably be a good idea to keep track of how often the stitch returns."

Spider glanced at his watch. "It's seven thirty."

"Good to know," Laurie murmured.

Ahead of them, Amy broke into a trot.

"She's going to break her neck," Spider said between his teeth.

"She's excited," Laurie said.

They tracked Amy's progress by way of her flashlight's erratic movements as she reached the pickup and climbed into the bed. "Ready?" she called.

"Do you know how to start the generator?" Spider called back.

Amy bent over with her light shining down. "Is this the one that Jack had?"

Spider and Laurie were just about there, and he waited to answer until he could speak in a normal tone. "Yes. His is quieter than mine, and I thought that'd be better."

"Then I know how to start it." Amy handed him her torch. "Can you hold this?"

As Spider held the light, Laurie asked, "Where is the star?"

"It's above us but a bit closer to the cliff face," Spider said. "You won't have a problem seeing it."

Amy straightened up and announced, "Everyone except Spider turn off your lights."

All complied, and the darkness pressed around them, pushed back by the golden circle in back of the pickup. Amy's movements were crisp and sure as she pushed two rocker switches and pulled on the starter rope. The generator sprang into life, and when it was running smoothly, she turned off the choke and plugged in the line that hung down from above.

Spider turned off his flashlight and looked up, blinking as Amy's star burst forth. She had fashioned it into a glowing orb with a major axis of shimmering light sticking through like a knitting needle stuck into a ball of yarn. Six smaller rays fanned out at different angles. It looked like something an artist would put on a Christmas card, a beautiful, gleaming starburst hanging in a black velvet sky.

Nobody spoke. They all stood silently, heads back, mouths open, eyes fixed on Amy's stellar stand-in.

Spider's throat constricted, and he felt a warm glow in his chest. He wiped his right eye with the heel of his hand to clear his vision and swallowed to get rid of the lump in his throat. When he could finally speak, his words were hushed, as if he were standing in a sacred place. "You were right, Amy. It truly is spectacular."

Amy's Star ~ 8

WHEN THE NIGHT became too chilly, they finally moved back to the stable, but Amy wouldn't hear of going inside. "Ben, you get the chairs, and Spider, you get the heater and bring it out here. I'll get the blankets. We can wrap up and look at the star while we listen to the Christmas story."

While Laurie stayed in the tack room to check on Goldie through a window into her adjacent stall, the rest of them arranged the chairs in a semi-circle around the propane heater. Amy spread the blankets out on the seats, and they all cocooned in the soft covers. When Laurie arrived, Amy pointed out her chair with the beam of her flashlight and then asked, "Isn't this cozy?"

"It's wonderful," Laurie said, slipping into her seat and turning off her light.

As everyone else doused their torches, Grace began to sing. Spider was amazed that such a full, honeyed contralto could come out of that frail-looking body. "Star of the east," she sang. "Thou Bethlehem star."

Ben joined her on the second line. His pure, sweet tenor blended perfectly with hers, creating a rich harmony that tightened Spider's throat again. He reached for Laurie's hand and held it until the last verse soared out into the night.

> *Star of the East, thou hope of the soul,*
> *While round us here the dark billows roll,*
> *Lead us from sin to glory afar,*
> *Thou star of the East, Thou sweet Bethlehem's star.*

When the song was over, Spider remained as he had been during the song, eyes on Amy's creation, Laurie's hand in his. He felt her squeeze his fingers.

"Are you going to read?" she whispered.

"Oh. Yeah."

"I brought out your Bible." Laurie disengaged and handed it to him. "And here's a penlight."

Spider took the small flashlight from her and turned it on. Then he fanned his scriptures open to the New Testament and flipped forward to the book of Luke. Putting the small pool of light on the beginning of Chapter Two, he read, "And it came to pass in those days, that there went out a decree from Cæsar Augustus—"

He stopped suddenly. Looking at Ben's shadowy form to his left, he said, "It starts before that." He paged backward to Matthew.

Now the birth of Jesus Christ was on this wise: When as his mother Mary was espoused to Joseph, before they came together, she was found with child of the Holy Ghost.

Spider read the story to the end, how Joseph had been stricken by the news of Mary's pregnancy and how an angel had appeared and told him to go ahead with the marriage. This was a holy child, the angel said, and Joseph was to be a father to him.

After finishing that chapter, Spider returned to Luke and began again.

With the penlight illuminating each line, he read through the ancient story of Joseph and Mary trying to find a place to stay and ending up in a stable where the baby was born. He read of the shepherds hearing the news from a heavenly choir and making haste to see, looking for a baby wrapped in swaddling clothes and lying in a manger. He finished with the verse about Mary keeping all the things that had happened and pondering them in her heart. Then he turned off the penlight and closed his book.

"Wait!" Amy's voice came from his right. "What about the star? You didn't read about the star."

"That was later, with the three wise men," Laurie said.

"No, Amy's right." Spider turned his flashlight back on. "I should have read about the star." He opened his Bible and, when he had found the passage, read about wise men coming from the east. When he finished the verse about the star showing where the Christ child was, Amy said, "Read that one again."

Spider obliged.

...and, lo, the star which they saw in the east, went before them, till it came and stood over where the young child was.

Amy sighed. "Can't you just picture it?"

"Your star helps," Spider said. "Now let me finish the next two verses." He read about the gifts of gold, frankincense and myrrh and how the three kings went home by a different way, so they didn't have to report to jealous Herod.

Spider turned off his penlight, and they all quietly contemplated their own star in the east until Grace gave a quick intake of breath. Spider looked at his watch and held it up so Laurie could see the luminous dial. It was eight fifteen.

Laurie turned on her torch and shone it on Grace. "How're you doing?"

Grace seemed to be trying to smile, but it was more of a grimace. "My stitch is back. Boy, it sure is persistent."

Ben rubbed her back. "Do you want to lie down for awhile?" He looked at Laurie. "Would that be all right?"

"Yes. I imagine you'd rather lie down in the house, even if it is dark. You can take your flashlights and one of the lanterns in with you, too, but—"

"But what?" Amy and Ben asked the question at the same time, both sets of eyes wide in the torchlight.

Laurie smiled. "It's nothing to worry about, but this could be the beginning of Grace's labor. It may stay in her back but will probably move around to her belly. When it does, keep track of when the contractions occur, and when they get to be two minutes apart, come and get us."

Ben stood. "Omygosh! Omygosh! Okay." He held up his hands and took a deep breath. "Two minutes. I've got that." He turned to Grace. "Let me help you up. Do you want me to carry you in?"

Grace laughed. "I just made it out to the star and back. I can make it to the house." But she let him help her out of the chair. Still wrapped in her blanket, she walked in the circle of his arm toward the house.

Laurie got up. "I'll go in and see that they're settled." She picked up Ben's blanket. "The house should stay warm for awhile, but I'll take this in just in case. Amy, could you get one of the lanterns from the tack room and bring it in for them?"

Amy stood. "Sure. And then I think I'm going to go to town. I want to see what the star looks like from there."

Spider smiled in the darkness. "I'll bet it looks spectacular."

"I'll bet it does, too." Amy turned on her flashlight and trotted off toward the stable while Laurie followed her own luminous circle to the house.

Spider sat alone, watching her light swinging as she walked. He ran his hand over the cover of his scriptures and sang softly, "Away in a manger, no crib for his bed."

Amy's Star ~ 9

WHILE LAURIE WAS getting Grace settled, Spider did some rearranging in the tack room, so he could set up the cots. He carried in the heater, brought in the chairs, and spread the blankets on the beds. The chairs he placed under the window that looked into Goldie's stall.

When everything was set up, Spider cupped his hands around his eyes to block out the lantern light as he pressed against the window and peered into the darkened stall. The palomino restlessly paced around the stall. They might be waiting all night for the foal.

Spider grabbed his flashlight and went to the shop again to search in the darkened storeroom for the place he had stashed the camp equipment. When he found it, he lifted down the camp stove and found the one-gallon coffeepot. He was glad that Jack had put a sink with running water in the tack room.

The pot clanked against the metal of the stove as he left the shop and carried them in one hand, his flashlight in the other.

Laurie opened the stable door as he approached. "If you're trying to sneak up on me, it isn't working," she said, giggling.

"I need more practice." Spider turned off his torch, tossed it on one of the cots, and handed the coffeepot to Laurie. "Would you fill this with water?"

Laurie took hold of the handle. "What're you going to do?"

"I thought you might like some hot chocolate while we're waiting on Goldie." Spider looked around for a surface to put the stove on.

"The stove can go on that bench outside Goldie's stall." Laurie set the pot in the sink and let water stream in. "This is a good idea. I'll go get the cocoa mix and some cookies."

Spider paused at the door. "How many cookies did you make this morning?"

"A couple hundred. I intended to spread them around town this afternoon. That was before the wounded birds and the Bethlehem star." She turned off the tap and followed Spider out the door with the water. Setting the pot on the bench, she turned on her flashlight for her return to the house.

◌

It was well after nine before Spider was finally in his chair with a cup of hot chocolate in his hands. "Aren't you going to sit down and drink yours?" he asked Laurie. "It's going to get cold."

She stood with her forehead against the window, looking into Goldie's stall.

He took a sip. "Is she doing all right?"

"So far. She's still in the first stage. Restless, you know? Down and up. I could use a strong lantern, though. When she finally decides to stay down, I want to be able to see that the foal is presenting properly."

Spider reached over and patted her on the leg. "Have your cocoa, and then I'll go get you one."

Laurie sighed and sat down. "I'm all of a sudden a little tired. Are you?"

"Haven't had time to think about it." He handed her a steaming cup. "It's been quite a Christmas Eve, hasn't it?"

Laurie chuckled. "I can't remember one quite like it."

As she put her cup to her lips, the door burst open.

Ben, eyes wide, stepped through the door, half supporting and half dragging Grace with him.

Spider jumped to his feet and felt Laurie's drink being thrust into his hands as he stared at the young people in the doorway. Neither had on a jacket, and Grace stood spraddle-legged. She was white as a sheet, and Ben was almost as pale.

Laurie was across the room in a second. "What's the matter? What happened?"

Grace began to cry. "It's coming. Oh, Laurie, I can't help it. It's coming. Right now."

Spider set the drinks in the sink. "Right now? How do you know? Haven't you been timing the contractions?"

"Yes, but they never got up to two minutes," Ben said. "They kept getting shorter instead."

"Never mind that," Laurie said grimly. "Help me get her on the cot."

Spider and Ben didn't have to be told twice. They picked Grace up and lay her down.

Laurie gave Ben and Spider a list of things to bring from the house, pronto. Ben was out the door in a moment, but Spider paused to ask, "What do you want the paper—"

"Now!" Laurie commanded.

Spider left. He had forgotten his flashlight but didn't want to go back for it, so he depended on the light of Amy's star to find his way to the kitchen door. Luckily, Ben had brought his torch, and he shone it on the counter, so Spider could grab the newspaper and make his way outside. He followed Ben as he dashed back across the pavers to the barn.

Amy was on the cot with her knees up and open. Her formerly pale face was now flushed as she kept her eyes on Laurie and kept repeating, "Hee, hee, hee, hoo."

"You're doing fine, dear," Laurie told her as she pulled a box of latex gloves from the cupboard. "Rest now until the next contraction, and then I'm going to let you push."

Laurie looked at the men, standing just inside the door with their burdens.

"Put your things on one of the chairs," she instructed. "Ben, you're to go to the kitchen and dial 9-1-1. Tell them to send an ambulance. The baby will probably beat them here, but tell them to hurry anyway."

Ben nodded and dashed away.

"Spider, my bathrobe is still in the dryer. Will you bring it to me? Take your flashlight this time, and hurry."

Spider saluted, grabbed his torch, and headed for the house again. As he made his way to the laundry room, he heard Ben on the phone.

"What do you mean you can't send anyone?" Ben sounded frantic. "There's a woman here having a baby. She's tiny and frail. No, the *woman* is tiny. The baby isn't here yet."

Spider yanked the dryer door open and dug around for Laurie's bathrobe. He saw a flash of pink, pulled it out, and sprinted to the back door. He reached it just as Ben hung up the phone. Was he crying?

When Spider got to the tack room, Laurie met him at the door. "We haven't much time. Put it on me. Backwards." She stuck out her arms, and when Spider slipped it on her, she turned around, so he could tie it in back. "Is your handkerchief clean? Let me have it."

Spider handed it to Laurie, and she folded it into a triangular shape. As she tied it around her head and underneath her hair, she said, "I'm going to need some dental floss and a pair of scissors. You'll find both in the top drawer in the bathroom. Underneath the sink there's a bottle of rubbing alcohol. Bring that, too."

"I'm on it," Spider said.

As he turned away, he heard Grace say, "Laurie?"

"I'm putting on my gloves, Gracey-love. It's time to get that Christmas baby here."

Spider closed the door behind him and started toward the house. He met Ben at the edge of the patio. "Are they going to send an ambulance?"

"They said the ambulance is out. There was a wreck up north of town. That's what took out the power." Ben's voice cracked. "I said I was going to bring her in myself, and they said don't. They're swamped with injured people from the accident." He took a deep breath and blew it out through his mouth. "They're getting hold of a home health nurse and sending her out."

Spider put his hand on Ben's shoulder. "Buck up, man. Laurie's as good as a home health nurse or a doctor for that matter. Why, she's delivered lots of critters."

"Critters?"

"Calves. Horses. Puppies. The process is the same, man. Grace is in good hands." He took off and called over his shoulder, "I've got to go get stuff for tying the cord."

As he went, he heard Ben mutter, "Critters."

At the house, Spider took the stairs two at a time. He got the things on his list as quickly as he could, though he had to get on his hands and knees to find the alcohol under the sink. Heading back, his torch went out in the upstairs hall. He swore under his breath and made his way gingerly down the stairs.

Ben met him at the bottom. "Laurie says she needs that stuff."

"Already? The baby's here?"

"Can you believe it? C'mon." Ben tugged at Spider's sleeve.

Spider took off, running in the backwash of Ben's light. Slamming through the back door, he sprinted across the pavers to the stable. At the door he skidded to a stop. "Here," he said to Ben. "You take it in."

Ben held up his hands and shook his head. "I'll wait until Grace's ready for me to see her."

Spider opened the door and stepped in. The newborn infant lay on an opened newspaper in front of Grace's flexed legs. Grace's eyes were closed, but the baby's were open. His arms and legs slowly moved in the air as he took stock of his new world.

"A son," Spider said, smiling. "A little boy."

"He's perfect," Laurie said.

"So why a newspaper?"

"If it hasn't been opened, it's probably the most sterile thing around. I figured I'd be wrapping him in it and sending him on his way in the ambulance. I guess we're going to Plan B." Laurie moved her attention from the baby as Grace's eyes sprang open, and she groaned.

"I'm out of here," Spider said. He opened the door and stepped into the cool, crisp air.

"Is everything all right?" Ben's anxiety showed in his voice.

"Everything's fine," Spider said. "It's a boy."

"A boy?" Ben looked like he was ready to reach for the doorknob.

"They're still busy in there." Spider jerked his head toward the shop. "Let's go see if we can find something to use for a bed."

Ben hesitated a moment before lighting their way, matching Spider's stride. Halfway to the shop, he said, "About the story you read tonight?"

"Yeah?"

"I've heard it before. Except for that part you read first, about Joseph."

"It gets overshadowed by the shepherds and the star."

"There was something in that story I never realized before."

Spider opened the door to the shop and turned to look at Ben.

"Yeah? What is that?"

"Joseph was a stepfather, too."

Amy's Star ~ 10

LATER THAT EVENING, Laurie and Spider sat in the cozy tack room with Grace and Ben and their new little boy. Spider had found a large plastic bin, and Ben had scrubbed and disinfected it while Spider fashioned a mattress out of a foam pad, a towel and a pillow case. The rude bassinet, unused as yet, sat by the cot. Grace held the infant in her arms as she lay propped up on pillows.

Laurie stood at the window, head pressed against the glass as she stared through into Goldie's stall. Spider sat in the chair next to her, facing the young couple.

Ben knelt beside Grace, his head bent over the bundle in her arms. As he touched the tiny hand, the baby's fingers curled around one of his own, and his voice grew husky. "What shall we name him?"

"Noel Latham Clark," Grace said.

Ben smiled at her. "Noel. It's perfect."

Needing something to occupy his attention, so he could give the young couple some privacy, Spider pulled out his pocketknife and picked up a short board he had brought in to block up the baby's bed. Though he kept his eyes on the shavings, he couldn't turn off his ears and was privy to the rest of the murmured conversation.

Grace spoke. "I was hoping we could be married before he came."

"That doesn't matter," Ben said. "I'm his dad whether he comes before or after the wedding."

Trey, sitting outside the stable door, began barking. The baby's arms jerked at the sudden noise, and he began fussing. Spider put down his whittling and sprang to the door to quiet the dog. As he stepped outside, Grace began to sing a lullaby.

Spider heard the slamming of car doors and peered into the darkness. He saw the corner of the breezeway lighten and then a flashlight beam came floating through. "Is that you, Amy?" he called.

"Shh," Amy replied in a hoarse stage whisper. "Don't say anything."

Spider waited silently for her to approach, and as she neared, he saw she wasn't alone. Two people followed behind her, and through the murky darkness, he could see one of them was shouldering a video camera.

The three paused outside the door as Grace's voice came floating through to them, still singing.

The story was told by the angels so bright,
As round them was shining a heavenly light.
The stars shone out brightly, but one led the way
And stood o'er the place where the dear baby lay.

Amy and the two visitors stood in the light that fell through the high tack room windows and allowed Spider a better view. The young woman with the camera was stocky with short, spiky hair and the glint of metal that must have been a piercing at her lip. The other was tall and willowy with high boots, a short skirt, and long blonde hair topped with a knit beret. She motioned Amy to open the door.

Spider wondered if he should interfere but decided against it. If the ladies were filming a Christmas video, he didn't want to get in their way. He'd keep a close watch, though, to make sure they didn't get pushy.

Amy swung the door wide and then stood blocking the way as she gaped at the sight before her.

Covered with a patchwork quilt, Grace leaned back on the pillows and cradled the baby in her arms. Though both Ben and Laurie looked up when the door opened, Grace kept her eyes on the babe as she sang.

The blonde haired girl slipped by Amy and whispered something to Ben. He looked at the camera and seemed to consider the request and then nodded. The blonde motioned the camera closer as Grace sang the last line and then, smiling serenely, raised her beautiful dark eyes to look straight into the lens.

"Cut," said the blonde. She looked at her watch and then spoke to all in the room. "Hi. I'm Claire, and this is Monty. We're students over at Dixie State, and we heard about someone over here hanging a star in the sky. We thought we'd do a segment on it and see if we could get KZUT to pick it up."

Monty took the camera off her shoulder and spoke to Claire. "We don't have much time for editing."

Claire nodded, and her eyes again swept the room. "We'd like to talk to you some more, but right now we've got to see if we can get this on the air." She appealed to Grace. "Is that all right with you? It will be a terrific Christmas story."

Grace's eyes went back to the baby asleep in her arms. "Yes."

Ben added, "His name is Noel Latham Clark."

"Got it," Claire said. "Come on, Monty. We've got work to do." She paused at the door. "We'll be back soon. We can do this in the car."

As the videographers left, Trey began to bark again. Spider watched through the doorway as a momentary halo shone around the house. Another car was pulling into the driveway. "We've got more company."

Laurie moved behind him and looked out. "We're not having the whole county traipsing in here to look at this baby."

"They're coming to see the star," Amy said. "You should see it from Kanab."

Spider grinned. "Spectacular?"

Amy grinned back. "More than spectacular. Amazing."

Laurie took hold of the door. "If the whole county is coming up, that's fine. We'll host them, but this little family isn't going to be bothered. They don't need every virus in Kane County being tracked in here."

"Come on, Amy," Spider said, scooting her out the door. "I'll build a fire, so people can warm themselves. You heat up the water for hot chocolate. Laurie, darlin', looks like people decided to come get their cookies since you didn't take them around."

Spider turned to greet the first arrival, a man wearing a gray hoodie. It turned out to be Hank, and Spider enlisted him to help build a fire in the old metal wheelbarrow. They used it for a portable fire pit and made some makeshift benches with boards and buckets.

"Don't make the fire too big," Amy said. "I don't want it to overshadow the star."

Hank broke a piece of kindling over his knee. "Nothing could overshadow your star." He pointed with the stick. "Look. You got two more cars coming up the driveway."

Amy practically danced. "It's just like the real Christmas story."

Laurie stepped out of the tack room and called, "We've had another advent."

Spider set down the load of firewood he was carrying. "What?"

"Come and see." Laurie walked to the adjacent stable door.

Amy squealed. "Goldie?" She jumped up and down and grabbed Hank, the nearest person, and gave him a hug. "Goldie had her baby."

"Who's Goldie?" Hank asked.

"She's a horse that came to visit." Amy took Hank's hand and dragged him over to join Laurie and Spider at the stable half-door.

Spider shined his light in the stall, and a sorrel colt that seemed to be all legs turned his head to stare at them.

"Oh, look," Amy said. "He's got a star on his forehead."

Laurie put an arm around her. "Another Christmas star."

Spider lowered the beam to the floor. "Can you tell about the hoof?"

"No." Laurie took hold of the top half of the stable door and started swinging it shut. "We need to leave them alone to bond," she said. "I'll check to see if it's deformed when I go in later."

"I'll bet it's going to be all right," Amy said. "This is a night made for miracles."

A sound fragment reached Spider's ears, so slight he wasn't sure he had heard anything. "Shhh. Listen," he said. Everyone quieted, and in the silence, there came a faint, "Hello? Anybody home?"

"Someone's at the front door," Amy said, grabbing Hank's hand again. "C'mon. Let's see who it is."

They clattered off, and the darkness swallowed them up. Laurie finished closing the stable door, and Spider latched it. Then he drew Laurie to him. "How're you doing?"

She leaned against his chest, and he felt her warmth as he breathed in her familiar scent.

"I'm fine," she said. "I don't know that I'm ready for more company, though."

Spider kissed her on the top of her head and then heard Amy holler, "It's the home health nurse."

"Thank heavens," Laurie said. "The cavalry has arrived."

Amy's Star ~ 11

SPIDER AND LAURIE walked together to greet the round, grandmotherly woman who slowly came through the breezeway with Amy on one side and Hank on the other.

She introduced herself as Mrs. Kingston and pointed her cane at Amy's creation hanging below the bluff. "I followed your star. It's like Fourth of July frozen in the sky."

Laurie laughed. "It's all Amy's doing. We're very glad it led you here."

"I don't get called out very often. I move a little slow, but I know babies." Mrs. Kingston waved her cane toward the lights of the tack room. "Is that where this new little one is? I'd better go take a look at him and his mother."

"We'll walk you over." As she and Hank continued with the nurse, Amy said over her shoulder, "There was another car pulling in. Better go rescue them."

"I'm on it," Spider said, striding across the pavers and through the breezeway. Rounding a corner, he almost collided with someone. Sensing, rather than seeing, a startled reaction, he heard a familiar voice say, "Spider?"

"Toby? Is that you?"

"Yeah. It's me."

"What're you doing back here? I thought you were up in Panguitch, popping the old question-a-roonie."

Toby didn't answer. He made a strangled sound, and then Spider felt himself being embraced by a sobbing, inarticulate deputy. Toby was weeping on his shoulder.

Spider patted him on the back, made soothing noises, and hoped that Toby had his own handkerchief. When the sobbing abated, Spider took him by the shoulders and pushed him back. "Would it help to talk about it?"

He heard Toby blow his nose, farmer style. That solved the handkerchief problem.

"Yes," Toby said damply.

Spider took him by the arm, shining a lighted circle in front of them to follow. "Come over to the fire," he said. "We won't be disturbed. The rest are in with the baby."

"Baby?"

"Yeah. Grace had her baby."

"Really? Where is she?"

"In the barn."

"Really?" Toby tripped over an uneven paver.

"Eyes on the ground," Spider admonished.

They made it the final fifty feet to the wheelbarrow fire pit. Spider turned off his lantern and sat on a bench, and Toby plopped down beside him.

"Now," Spider said. "Spill the beans."

"What beans?"

"The girl-in-Panguitch beans."

Toby sighed. His shoulders drooped, and he pulled the ring box out of his jacket pocket and fiddled with the lid. "I guess I won't be needing this now."

"Take it back to the store," Spider suggested. "Get your money back."

"Can't. I bought it on Ebay." Toby flipped the lid open, revealing an engagement ring and wedding band. "The diamond's not very big, but I didn't think she was the kind of a girl that would care about that."

Spider picked up a stick and pushed an ember back in the fire. "Did she turn you down flat?"

Toby cleared his throat. "I never got the chance to ask her," he said in a constricted voice. "She'd invited another fellow down from Salt Lake for Christmas. He works in computers."

Spider laid his hand on Toby's shoulder. "Well, we're glad to have you here with us. We've had all kinds of things going on today. Amy's star. Ben and Grace's little boy. And Goldie had a colt."

Toby leaned back, eyes wide. "Goldie? The horse you're keeping for—" He wagged his thumb over his shoulder as if that would supply the missing name.

"Yeah. Cute little sorrel."

"Is his hoof all right?"

"Don't know yet. Laurie wants to give them a chance to bond before she starts invading their space."

"Makes sense." Toby looked at the ring set and sighed. Then he closed the lid and put the box back in his pocket.

Someone called from the breezeway. "Amy? Mr. or Mrs.? Anybody?"

Toby turned toward the sound. "Who's Mr. or Mrs. Anybody?"

"I think she means me." Spider called out, "Over here." He went to light the way, and as he approached, he saw it was the video duo who had arrived earlier. "We're over by the fire," he said. "Did you get your editing done already?"

Monty, the stocky cameraperson, answered him. "The result of good camerawork. We not only got it done, but the boss lady herself is going to look at it.

"You don't say!" Spider led the two women to where Toby stood by the fire. "This is Toby Flint," he said by way of introduction. "Toby, meet Claire and Monty. They're journalism students who heard about Amy's star and came to see it."

Toby laughed. "Really?" Turning, he asked the girls, "Who told you about the star?"

"My grandma lives here in Kanab," Claire said. "Her neighbor's husband works at the hardware store, and he said some crazy lady came in and said President Obama told her to make a replica of the Bethlehem star."

Toby didn't respond, and in the flickering firelight, Spider read discomfort on his face.

The silence stretched out, and Claire said, "What? Did I say something wrong?"

"Think about it, Claire." Monty's voice had a hint of exasperation in it. "The fact that we're sitting right under the star is a clue that the person who made it lives here." Monty turned to Spider. "The segment is really quite nice. Would you like to see it?"

"Sure," Spider said. "How're we going to manage that with the power off?"

"I've got it on my tablet. Let's sit down." She sat on the bench in front of the fire and tapped an arrow on the screen.

Spider sat beside her and watched the image become a lighted street that looked like Kanab. The off-camera narrator—probably Claire—explained that they had heard someone was erecting a star in the vicinity, and they had come to find it. "They said the star was east of Kanab. We're heading that way."

As the car followed the ninety-degree bend at the junction, the brightly illuminated Samco service station went dark along with the rest of the town.

"That's weird," Claire mumbled on camera. "Do they turn off the electricity at nine every night?"

They continued driving east, finally reaching the inky edge of town where the highway climbed a knoll. As they gained the top, they were suddenly able to see what had been hidden before, a dazzling, Christmas-card star hanging low on the eastern horizon.

"Holy Toledo," Claire said in a hushed voice as the car pulled over and stopped.

"Look." It was Monty's voice now on the video. "Some people are out here watching the star." There was the hum of a window going down and then her voice, calling, "Excuse me. Could we talk to you?"

A man in a light colored hoodie came to the open window. In the darkness, his features were obscured.

The question was Claire's. "What do you know about that star?"

"I know it's spectacular," the man said.

Spider chuckled.

"Who put it up?" Claire asked.

"A very talented individual."

"We heard it was a crazy lady who was saying that President Obama told her to recreate the Bethlehem star."

"Well, I don't know if it was President Obama, but I saw someone in a big, black, stretch limo stop and talk to a friend of mine." He pointed to the star. "Judge for yourself whether she's crazy."

Spider touched Monty on the arm. "Will you play that again? What that fellow said?"

"Sure." She backtracked and played the segment about the crazy lady. "Is that what you wanted?"

"Yeah. Thanks," Spider said. His throat felt tight again, and he had a warm feeling around his heart. Ol' Hank. Good man.

"Let's see the rest," Toby said.

Monty tapped the arrow, and the image of the star stayed in the middle of the screen as they traveled up what sounded like a gravel road. Claire's voice became tentative, maybe a little scared, as they drove through the dark, finally reaching the house.

The next scene was a picture of the stable with the star above it, and then the camera approached the door. Spider heard Amy whispering they needed to be quiet, and then she was in the frame, opening the door to the tack room as Grace's voice floated to them singing the lullaby.

Spider sucked in a breath when the camera discovered Grace. She looked like a Madonna, cradling the child in her arms and gazing down upon it as she sang, unaware the lens was recording her every move. She looked up, gazed into the camera, and smiled serenely. Then the screen went dark.

"Wow," Toby said. "Wow."

Monty hugged the tablet. "Did you like it?"

"It was all great," Toby said. "I'd like to see it again, but I think we've got more visitors. Don't go away."

Spider gave Toby the flashlight. "You're the official greeter." He watched the deputy head toward the breezeway and then turned to Claire. "Can I put you in charge of cookies and hot chocolate?"

Claire agreed, and after Spider showed her where things were, he walked to the firelight's edge to greet the most recent visitors. It turned out to be Bishop Shaefer and his family.

Spider shook hands all around, and Toby herded the group over to the benches, so Monty could play the video for them.

Spider walked to the barn and poked his head in the tack room, asking for help with visitors. Hank and Amy came out, and he gave them the task of getting lights out front using some of Amy's unused lights, a battery, and an inverter. When they were gone, Spider stepped inside the cozy stable room.

Grace was sitting up in one of the camp chairs, cocooned in the patchwork quilt. Mrs. Kingston sat beside her with Laurie and Ben occupying the other seats. The baby slept in his makeshift bed sitting atop a bale of hay.

Spider paused to gaze at the tiny new being asleep with one little fist up by his cheek. Laurie joined him, and he put his arm around her waist. "Is that my sock you've got on his head?" he whispered.

"I cut off the top to make a cap. The rest of it is still in your drawer."

"I take comfort in that," he murmured. "By the way, we're getting lots of company out there. What's Bishop Shaefer's wife's name?"

"Are they here? Um, it's Vereen, I think."

"She works in the courthouse, doesn't she? Do you know where?"

"She's the county clerk." She cocked an eyebrow at him. "Why do you want to know?"

Spider winked at her. "Amy said this was a night made for miracles."

Amy's Star ~ 12

AS THE EVENING progressed, more and more townspeople arrived. They did a lot of talking about the accident up by Orderville that took out the substation and sent six people to the hospital. But they talked even more about the star. Everyone wanted to tell where they were when they first spied it.

And they talked about the wedding. Spider heard the whispering as the news was passed around. "Vereen went down and opened the office, so they could have a marriage license. Bishop Shaefer's gonna officiate when they get back." He heard cell phone conversations as the news went out over the airwaves. They usually ended with, "Just follow the star."

The more practical minded brought chairs, firewood and portable fire pits, and blankets to wrap up in. Soon the vast paved area behind the house was dotted with groups of people clustered around flickering fires. A child began singing "Away in a Manger," and others joined in.

They had just finished the song when Toby burst through the breezeway hollering, "They're back." He held up his torch to spotlight Vereen and Ben as they came through. A cheer went up, and Toby announced, "As soon as Bishop Shaefer and the bride are ready, we'll have the—" He broke off and looked up.

The throbbing thwick-thwick-thwick of a helicopter's rotors sounded loudly in the darkness, and Spider scanned the sky to locate it.

A little boy shouted, "There it is!" Everyone turned in the direction he was pointing as the airship became visible over the house.

"I hope he doesn't get too close to that line going to the top of the cliff," Spider muttered.

Laurie asked, "What does it say on the side? KZUT? Did Amy's star make the news?"

The helicopter disappeared behind the house again, and Spider took Laurie's hand and led her through the breezeway. "It may have. Monty sent it in."

They reached the driveway, and they could see the helicopter hovering over the alfalfa field below them. Toby dashed out, hollering, "I'll go light the field for them." He hopped in his car and tore out of the driveway with Hank and Amy right behind him.

"Holy Toledo!"

Spider wheeled around to see who had spoken and found Claire beside him.

"What is it?"

"That's Kathryn Engle, executive producer and powerhouse at KZUT. I've got to get down there."

As Claire held up her cell phone to light her way to her VW, Laurie said, "Kathryn Engle is also Grace's mother. Now the fat's in the fire."

They stood and watched as the two pickups bumped over the field to light a landing area, and the helicopter set down between them.

Laurie linked her arm through Spider's. "Do you suppose she saw the piece Monty sent in?"

"I think it's pretty certain."

"Well, at least she already knows about the baby. How'd she get here so fast?"

"Beats me. She must have been pretty far south doing news things and just came on over when she recognized her daughter." Spider tugged on Laurie's arm. "We'd better go let Grace know her mother'll be at her wedding."

Amy's Star ~ 13

WHEN THEY TOLD Grace that her mother was on the way up the driveway, she grew pale, and her hand went to her throat. "I don't want to see her until I'm Mrs. Clark," she said, taking Ben's hand.

Laurie looked at Spider. "I vote that you're the one to tell her. I'll stay in here with Grace."

Spider snorted. "Mrs. Kingston can take care of Grace."

"She can't walk out with her for the ceremony," Laurie countered.

"I want Spider to walk out with me," Grace said. "I want him to give me away."

Spider sent a triumphant glance Laurie's way.

Grace added, "But I think he should be the one to tell my mother how things stand."

A knock sounded at the door. "Spider," Toby called. "Kathryn Engle is here and wants to talk to Grace."

Grace's brown eyes were large as she looked up at Spider. He read in them a plea for help, and he sighed. "Okay. Give me five minutes, and then let's get this wedding under way." Opening the door just wide enough to slip though, he stepped outside and confronted the powerhouse at KZUT.

She was tall, almost as tall as Spider. Shoulder length blonde hair in an elegant cut framed a handsome face with a jaw that seemed set. She had the same large eyes as Grace, but hers were steel gray and looked like they had had a lot of practice in seeing through subterfuge.

"Good evening, Ma'am. I'm Spider Latham. I'm, uh..." He looked around at the crowd gathered in the back yard, many of them staring at the woman who had come in a helicopter. "Let's talk someplace else."

He led her along Hank and Amy's luminous path through the breezeway and out onto the front drive. With the beam of his flashlight, he indicated the low wall that ran along the far side. "Would you care to sit a minute?"

She didn't sit. "Don't think you can charm me with your aw-shucks, Jimmy Stewart imitation," she said in clipped accents. "I've come to get my daughter and take her home."

Spider turned off his flashlight and gazed up at Amy's star, searching his mind for something to say. Trying to defuse her anger, he said, "Home means different things to different people."

"Home is home." Her voice allowed no opposition.

"Yeah, but if it turns out that home's not a safe place anymore, then maybe it becomes something else."

"What are you saying?" Her voice cut through the darkness like a switchblade.

"The Princeton man? The one you insisted she go out with?"

Silence.

She finally sat on the wall.

When she spoke, all the steel had gone out of her voice. "I did this to her."

"Good things are coming from it, Mrs. Engle. Ben's a good man, and she loves him."

She sniffed but said nothing.

Spider went on. "Ben will raise the boy as his own. He's studying to be an electrician, and he'll be able to provide for her well."

"An electrician." She spoke as if she had bit into something bitter. "I wanted her to marry a lawyer."

Spider turned on his flashlight and swept it in an arc over the valley below. "Earlier this evening there were lights scattered all over down there. You could see the lights of Kanab over by that point. Right now, who do you think those people would rather see? An electrician or a lawyer?"

Silence. Then a sigh. "All right." Finally, she stood. "When I got here, people were talking about a wedding. I understand the bride is my daughter."

"Yes. Shall we go? It's about to start." Spider led her back through the breezeway.

Halfway to the festive back yard, she linked her arm through his and said, "I insist on a front row seat."

Amy's Star ~ 14

SPIDER AND LAURIE waved to the last of their guests, and he put his arm around her as they walked back to the benches where Amy sat alone.

Spider threw another log on the fire and stood watching it begin to burn. "What an evening!"

"It was a magical night," Laurie said. "I think the most magical time was when Bishop Shaefer asked about a ring, and Toby pulled that little box out of his pocket."

He chuckled. "Yeah, ol' Toby. He did all right."

Hearing a door close, Spider looked toward the barn and saw a light coming toward them. When it got closer, he recognized Ben and his new mother-in-law.

"Mrs. Kingston is helping Grace with Noel's feeding," Ben said. "We thought we'd come out here and wait." He paused while Mrs. Engle took a seat and then sat on a different bench.

"How is Grace doing?" Laurie asked. "Did the wedding tire her out?"

"A little, but she's doing fine." Ben held his hands to the fire. "How is your colt? Did you check his hoof?"

"I did." Laurie smiled. "He's perfect."

At that moment, the lights flickered and came on. The halogen on top of the garage and the one on top of the barn cast shimmering circles that intersected where the little group sat around the fire. The windows of the house glowed in the dark, spilling light out onto the patio in trapezoidal bricks.

"Ooooh," Amy moaned. "The magic is gone."

"Well, the magic may be gone, but the furnace is on, and we'll have a warm place to sleep tonight." Laurie stood. "Mrs. Engle, may I show you to your room? I hope you won't mind sharing with Mrs. Kingston. You'll have twin beds, and it's right next to Grace and Ben's room."

Ben got up. "I'll come with you. If Mrs.—I mean Mother Engle—wants to shower, I'll carry the water out for her."

Mrs. Engle paused and looked from Laurie to Spider, a frown on her face.

"We've got drain problems," Spider said. "Ben will explain about all the complications."

"And he'll show you where the porta-potty is," Amy added.

Mrs. Engle stared at Spider for a moment, and then a smile lifted the edges of her mouth. "I suppose you're going to ask me whether I'd rather see a plumber right now or a lawyer?"

Spider answered her smile. "It crossed my mind."

Mrs. Engle looked up at Amy's star and then reached her hand out to her son-in-law. "Come with me, Ben, and show me what you're worth."

Spider watched them walk hand in hand toward the house behind Laurie. "You got it right, Amy. It's a night made for miracles."

Other books by Liz Adair

Trouble at the Red Pueblo, #4 in the Spider Latham Mystery Series (Also set in Kanab, Utah)
Snakewater Affair, #3 in the Spider Latham Mystery Series
After Goliath, #2 in the Spider Latham Mystery Series
The Lodger, #1 in the Spider Latham Mystery Series
The Mist of Quarry Harbor
Cold River
Lucy Shook's Letters from Afghanistan
Hidden Spring, a novella in the *Timeless Romance, Old West Collection*

About Liz Adair

A native of New Mexico and mother of seven, Liz Adair bloomed late as a writer. Though she lived in green, moist, northwest Washington State for forty years, most of her books are set in the southwest. Liz returned to high plateau country in 2012 when she and her husband, Derrill, moved to Kanab, Utah.

Liz had gone to high school in Kanab and neighboring Fredonia, Arizona, so moving there was like coming home. It was natural for her next book to be another Spider Latham mystery, even though ol' Spider hadn't inhabited one of her books for ten years. Writing about him again felt like coming home, too, and a Christmas story at the Latham's was like Christmas with an old friend.

Look for more books set in Kanab coming out this year. You can check out Liz's blog at **www.sezlizadair.blogspot.com** and be sure to sign up for her newsletter to find out about new releases.

At Whit's End

by

Terry Deighton

Terry's Acknowledgements

Many thanks to the village that worked on this book. My critique group, which deserves more gratitude than I can express for their patience, expertise, and encouragement, includes Liz Adair, Ann Acton, Bonnie Harris, Tanya Parker Mills and Christine Thackeray. My beta readers helped hone and polish the story. Thanks to Kat Rozenbaum, Colleen Deighton, Crystal Deighton, and Rebecca Barrett.

At Whit's End ~ 1

NOT WANTING TO put her husband on the spot in front of the real estate agent, Whitney Saunders simply caught Nick's eye and gave him a nod. Her subterfuge had evidently failed because the realtor said, "I'm going to return a call to another client and let you two talk." She stepped a few paces away and pulled out her cell phone.

Whitney gave her husband the puppy dog look that had always worked on her father. "What do you think?"

His face remained blank. "I said I'd look at houses, Whit. I didn't say we could buy. I'm on probation until my four month review." He sighed. "We can't count on my job, let alone a raise, yet."

She gazed up at him with the full force of her longing. "Nick, you know you'll keep the job and get the raise. You graduated cum laude. They practically begged you to take the position."

"But this is the best accounting firm in Seattle. I need to concentrate on the job, not a house. We should rent for a year or two and save up."

"We'd be so happy here." She stroked his arm. "The sun room's northern exposure would make it a wonderful art studio, and there's plenty of room for when children come."

He eyed the house. "It *is* a good house, but it would take all our money for a down payment even if we could get them to come down a few thousand dollars."

He was thinking about it. Whitney concentrated on arguments that would appeal to her accountant husband. "We've been preapproved for more than the asking price. You can draw up a strict budget. I'll follow it; I promise." She peered into his eyes. "This house speaks to me in a language I can't translate into words."

"There'd be no money for decorating or improvements."

"It doesn't need improvements, and I can wait for curtains and such. I promise not to fuss about waiting."

His furrowed brow reminded her how reluctant he'd been to get married in the middle of their junior year instead of waiting for graduation. She'd won him over with a smoldering kiss. She eyed the realtor a few feet away. Maybe this time she'd better appeal to his practical nature. "It will actually make us money in the long run."

The sudden rise of his eyebrows spurred her on.

She cast around her mind for convincing arguments. "We won't have the expense of moving in, connecting the utilities and all that, twice if we move directly from the motel to the house."

He didn't seem convinced, so she plumbed the depths of the financial mumbo jumbo she'd helped him study all those months. "The interest is tax deductible while rent is not, so our taxes will be lower."

He screwed his mouth up the way he always did while figuring out a problem. She had him on the run. "Besides, this place is close to both our jobs. It won't cost nearly as much for gas and car maintenance. And since we'll be close, I can pick up extra shifts at the craft store when they need someone on short notice."

That did it. She could see the mental calculations flying behind his eyes.

His face took on a faraway look. "If we can get them to come down ten thousand dollars, then..."

He'd switched from could to can. She'd won. Whitney turned, so the realtor couldn't see the grin on her face. "You mean we can buy it?"

Nick reached out and tucked her hair behind her ear. "Maybe. If they'll come down, I think we can swing it, but don't get your hopes up." He looked down at her. "There won't be *any* money for extras until after I get my first raise."

She felt like a scolded child, but she wouldn't let that get to her. Instead, she concentrated on his willingness to please her. Of course the seller would come down. Hardly anyone pays the asking price. She breathed in the crisp fall air. They were finally going to have their own home.

She stopped herself from throwing her arms around Nick's neck and giving him a big kiss. She wanted him to be able to keep his poker face. He'd have better leverage if the woman couldn't use his wife's enthusiasm against him.

Even though she couldn't trust herself to hide her emotions, she could trust Nick to make the best deal. She patted his arm, leaving him to talk to the woman and shuffled through the red and golden leaves across the front lawn to the agent's car. There, she retrieved her artist's pad and pencil set from the backseat and positioned herself to sketch their new home. She drew light lines to block in the shape, paying little attention to the conversation behind her. Whatever the cost or the sacrifice, they were going to build something wonderful together in this place.

She added in the windows and gabled peaks, including the little dormer of the perfect room for a nursery. As the agent dialed her phone again, Whitney angled to the left, so she could see the realtor's face. It looked hopeful. She must think Nick's offer would be accepted. Whitney's heart beat faster. If they could buy this house, she wouldn't miss home and family so much.

The agent looked up from her phone. "I'll put the offer in right now. My office represents the seller, so that should speed things up." The realtor held the phone to her ear but continued to talk to Nick. "With your combined income, there shouldn't be a problem. I do wish you weren't both so new to your companies, though. You've only been there a few days."

"Don't forget," Nick said, "our savings and our parents graduation presents add up to thirty thousand to put down."

The agent smiled and nodded but held up a finger to signal that her office had answered. Whitney tuned out the woman's clipped tones and concentrated on her drawing, giving definition to the rooflines and adding the charming wood trim around the gables. Then she drew what she already thought of as her studio jutting out from the dining room. Working part-time at the craft store in the mall should give her plenty of time to draw and paint, and she'd be learning to frame her own work, too.

Her dad had harrumphed when she'd told him about her new job. He'd asked her, repeatedly, not to major in art. "You'll never be able to make enough to support yourself," he'd said as often as he'd told her not to walk home from campus at night by herself. With Nick's income, it wouldn't matter if she sold much. She could create pieces that meant something.

"Right, Whit?"

"Sorry, what?"

"If they accept our offer, we could sign papers tomorrow at five. You'll get off work in time."

"Yes." She finally let her joy show on her face. "That would be fine."

Maybe she should pay more attention to the financial details, but the aesthetics of the house compelled her to continue her drawing. She studied the bay window of the living room. She could almost see a Christmas tree twinkling behind the glass. Without thinking much about it, she added the tree then penciled in strings of lights along the gutters.

Christmas in their own home would make up for being three thousand miles away from either of their families, and when she finished this drawing, it would make the perfect Christmas card.

At Whit's End ~ 2

THANKSGIVING FOUND WHITNEY in her new kitchen, removing a turkey from the oven and replacing it with a pan of brown and serve rolls. "Come and carve the bird," she called to Nick. "Dinner's almost ready." She went to the fridge and took out Grandma Saunder's famous fruit salad, a surprise for her husband. The first holiday in their first real home needed to blend the best of both families' traditions.

Nick's arms appeared around her in a bear hug, and he nuzzled her neck with his nose. "Mmmm. It sure smells good in here."

"Do you mean me or the food?"

"Both. I'm starving." He stuck his finger in the bowl, scooping up some salad and sticking it in his mouth before she could slap his hand away. He made a show of chewing the food and swallowing. "Hey, is that my grandma's salad?"

Whitney grinned. "Yes. I got the recipe from your mom last week." She peered up at him. "Does it taste right?"

"It's perfect, just like my wife." He hugged her to him again and kissed her behind the ear. "If I wasn't so hungry, I'd suggest another kind of feast."

She scooted away from him and put the salad on the counter that divided the kitchen from the dining room. "Save that thought for later. We're not letting anything ruin this meal. I've worked all week on it."

"Don't worry. I'll do it justice." He looked across the counter to the table. "Did you decide to invite someone after all? You've made enough food for the whole neighborhood."

"No, it's just us. Maybe next year we'll have someone over." She thought about last Thanksgiving with her family. Her sister's three kids had run wild, and there hadn't been a moment's peace. "I wanted today to be the two of us. We've spent every holiday since we got married with our folks. It's time we started our own traditions."

"It looks like one of our traditions is going to be eating leftovers for a week after Thanksgiving."

Whitney moved to the dining room while Nick sliced off several pieces of white and plenty of dark meat. He placed the platter on the counter and came around into the dining room. "Wow! This table belongs on the cover of *Better Homes and Gardens*. Look at those little Pilgrims and that pumpkin turkey. How much of your paycheck did you spend at the store this week?"

"Not much, really. I waited until it was marked down. With my employee discount—"

"Okay. I was teasing. You've kept your promise to stick with the budget." He gave her a hug and eyed the table again. "It looks wonderful. Let's eat."

Whitney moved toward the table then stopped, sniffing the air. "The rolls!" She darted around into the kitchen and threw open the oven door. Whiffs of smoke escaped, carrying a burnt smell.

Nick came up behind her. "They aren't too bad." He tapped one, causing a resounding thunk. "Not so you'd play hockey with them." He grabbed a hot pad and pulled the pan out of the oven. "We can cut the bottom part off and eat the tops."

"No." Whitney scowled. She'd worked so hard on this dinner. She took the hot pad, pan and all, and scraped the rolls into the garbage. "Who ruins brown and serve rolls?"

"No worries." Nick shut the oven and led her out of the kitchen. "As long as there's stuffing, we're all set."

Whitney looked at her beautiful table, only slightly less so now, and decided to shrug off the disappointment. "Well, the stuffing should be fine." She put on a smile and started in on the speech she'd been planning. "I thought we'd keep some traditions from each of our families." She pointed to the salad. "We have Grandma Saunder's salad, and I thought we'd hold hands and say a blessing like my folks do. Then we each say something we're thankful for."

"I remember." Nick made a show of breathing in the steamy fragrance of the food and pouted for a moment before grinning at her. "You say the blessing."

When she finished, she said she was thankful they could spend the holidays in their own house.

Nick looked around the table. "I'm most thankful for my beautiful, talented wife."

Whitney smiled at him, but her heart sank. She should have said she was thankful for Nick, not the house. Maybe she should explain though it didn't seem to bother him as evidenced by the way he shoveled food onto his plate. Still, she wanted him to understand. "It's that the house symbolizes us. Being thankful for being together in the house is the same as being thankful for you, for our marriage."

Nick handed her the potatoes. "I know, honey. It means a lot to you to be settled. I knew you meant being in the house with me." He poured gravy on his mound of potatoes then shifted to smother his dressing, too. "I know how women are. My mother always made sure the holidays were special."

That's was her job, now. The thought raced through Whitney's mind, engendering a thousand others. The kind of holidays they had would depend on her, and Christmas was only a month away. She didn't want another disaster like the burned rolls. She'd make this the best Christmas either of them ever had. She'd make their favorite treats, find a way to decorate the house, get Nick the perfect present.

Wait. The perfect present would *be* the perfect Christmas. She needed more information. "What did your mom do to make Christmas special?"

He sat back for a moment, chewing on her question along with his turkey. After swallowing, he said, "She made tons of cookies. I love those little white ball-shaped ones. And fudge. She always saved Grandma's fruitcake for Christmas Day."

Russian tea cakes. Fudge. Fruitcake. She could do that.

"And she took us to see Santa at the mall."

She added Santa to her mental list.

"She put a wreath on the door, and we always put up the tree a week before Christmas and decorated it together."

Wreath. Decorate the tree together.

As he talked, her mental to-do list grew until she made an excuse to hurry to the bedroom and write it all down. Thanksgiving came late in the month this year. She had less than four weeks, and it would take every minute.

At Whit's End ~ 3

THE NEXT DAY, Black Friday in the retail world, Whitney arrived at work at ten o'clock full of plans for the perfect Christmas, but the craft store had become a battle zone.

She blithely edged around the melee, heading for the relative calm of the frame shop, but a frenzied shopper grabbed her arm. "You work here, right? The ad shows this ribbon in red and green stripes, but all you have is solid colors."

The woman shoved her fully loaded shopping cart in front of Whitney, blocking her way. "I know it's a busy day, but, really, you should have what's in the ad."

Whitney plastered on her be-patient-with-the-customers smile. "I'm sure we had the striped ribbon, but we may be out. Let me check on it for you." She spotted Paige stocking the jingle bells half way down the aisle. Guiding the woman's cart that direction, she pulled its driver along.

As they approached, Whitney turned the cart, sandwiching it between herself and the irate customer. Paige looked up expectantly, and Whitney showed her the ad. "Can you check if we have any of this ribbon in the green and red stripe? Thanks." Not waiting for a reply, she ducked around a display of Christmas ornaments and took off her smock. No use advertising that she worked here until she had to.

At the back of the store, she slipped into the frame shop and her smock. The morning sped by as she worked on matting and framing five identical portraits of a smiling extended family—Christmas presents for the grown children in the photo, no doubt. She spent her break and lunch mapping out a calendar for accomplishing all her plans. If she stuck to it, she'd have everything ready in time.

After work, she walked down the mall to Santa's Workshop. Dodging a frantic mother in hot pursuit of twin toddlers, she made her way to the elf out front. "Who schedules private visits from Santa?"

The young woman in a pointed ears and a hat to match nodded. "Me. My Santas cover the mall, but I also schedule outside gigs for them."

"Great! Do you have anyone still available for Christmas Eve?"

No elf should ever make such an ugly face. "Christmas Eve? I doubt it. Most of my Santas are booked a year in advance for that night." She pulled her costume sleeve down, covering a rosebud tattoo, and went back to filling a basket with candy canes.

Whitney had clung to good will all day even amid Black Friday rudeness, but the elf's callous scuttling of her Christmas plan finally broke her determination. "Could you check, please?" Her irritation showed in her tone, so she added, "It's really important to me."

Santa's helper looked heavenward. "It always is." She took a cell phone out of her tunic and, with her mouth turned down, tapped at the screen with her glitter-encrusted acrylic nails.

"I'll look, but I'm sure—ooooh, I hadn't thought of *him*." She raised one shoulder, and her mouth looked as if it couldn't decide whether to smile or grimace. "I've got a new fellow this year, so he doesn't have repeat customers. He's available for the six o'clock hour." She glared at Whitney. "But that's it. It's the only slot available."

"That's perfect. I'll take him."

Elfie cocked her head as if to say, "Of course you will." Out loud, she rambled off an obviously memorized spiel. "That's twenty dollars now and another thirty at the end of the visit. There's an extra charge for more than six kiddos."

"It's for my husband, no children."

The elf wrinkled her forehead then shrugged. "Whatever."

Whitney ignored the comment. "It won't take the whole hour. Can I book him for half an hour?"

The elfish eyebrows shot up. "You're lucky to get him at all. It's fifty bucks an hour with a half hour travel time between gigs." She held her finger over the phone. "Take it or leave it."

The ultimatum almost pushed Whitney to snap, "Leave it," but the thought of disappointing Nick overcame her irritation, and she pulled a twenty out of her wallet. Maybe she could sell a piece of art to make up the difference.

Nick had been very firm in budgeting for December. She remembered the warning look he'd given her when he said, "Remember, we agreed to curtail spending when we bought the house." She knew from his firm tone he meant to remind her that it had been *her* idea to buy the house.

He'd softened slightly as he continued. "We'll spend fifty dollars on gifts for each set of parents and no more than fifty dollars for each other." Her dejection had evidently shown on her face because he hugged her and added, "Christmas will be great as long as we're together."

When she'd asked about Christmas decorations, he'd thrown in another twenty-five dollars but that would be instead of going out to dinner in December.

The Santa visit would eat up all the money she had for Nick's gift. Then she still needed to get something for the jolly old elf to pull out of his bag, some stocking stuffers, and special ingredients for the goodies Nick had mentioned. Then it hit her. How could she pay for printing her Christmas cards?

She'd thought when they graduated and got jobs, their money problems would be over. Of course, things wouldn't be so tight if they hadn't bought the house, but they'd be living in some apartment listening to the neighbors' parties and fights. The house was worth it. She'd have to find a way to turn her talent and education into some extra money like some of her classmates had.

A Christmas card had come the day before from one of her friends from school. Kara had started a nice little business drawing pet portraits in Miami since graduating last year. She'd included her price list and encouraged Whitney to do something similar.

If she could find a way to sell her work, Whitney felt sure Nick wouldn't care how she spent the extra money. She pondered the question all the way home and through the evening. When they went to bed, it poked her awake every time she relaxed enough to drift toward sleep. Nick's breathing finally slowed and settled into the not quite snore she loved, and still, she lay there, thinking about Christmas and how to pay for it all.

Her mind started updating her to-do list. Tomorrow she needed to figure out what to get their parents since it had to be shipped. If she got gift cards, they could go in the Christmas card envelopes at no extra cost. Christmas cards! She needed to make them before she could even think about including anything in the envelopes. Going to the office supply store to copy her drawing onto cardstock went on the list.

Again, her mind circled back to using her art to get the rest of the fee for Santa. Could she consign some of her college work at a local gallery? Even if she did, she'd never get the money soon enough.

Maybe she could get gift cards for their parents at a discount somehow and use the extra money for Santa. Her groggy mind returned to the cards she needed to make.

The two ideas blended to form a solution.

She could make drawings of their parents' houses and frame them herself. There were some very nice, special order picture frames at work that had been returned by a customer. The store couldn't send them back, so she figured the manager would sell them to her at a discount. She could mail them in padded envelopes to minimize shipping costs. It should save her enough to pay for everything she'd planned. Besides, what better gift could they give their parents than pictures of the homes they'd raised their children in?

She started mentally blocking in her parents' house. This was ridiculous. She might as well get up and do it for real. She'd only work for a little while, just long enough to lay out the basic shapes.

She had to hunt through a box to find pictures of both their houses. Then she spent time sketching the outline of her parents' place. Examining her work, she decided it would be a much better present than a gift card to Applebee's. Looking at the clock shocked her. She'd been up over an hour.

Whitney crawled back into bed, careful not to disturb Nick. As she drifted off to sleep, she had the thought that she wouldn't tell him about the drawings for their parents until they were done and framed. It would be one more little Christmas surprise.

At Whit's End ~ 4

THE ALARM SHRILLED Whitney awake the next morning. It took several moments before her brain cleared enough for her to figure out it was Saturday. She rolled over and snuggled into her pillow. Then the reality of her retail job hit home. She had an hour to get to work.

During the day, she dragged herself from one task to the next. Why was she so tired? Of course, she'd gotten up to work on the sketches. The minute she thought of them, she felt energized. A few more nights would have her parents' house finished. Then she could work on Nick's childhood home.

Of course, if she told him her idea, she could work on them in the evenings. No, if he knew she was spending so little on their parents' gifts, she'd have to tell him why she still needed the money he'd budgeted. Better to work while he slept.

Since neither she nor Nick had to work the next day and could sleep in, she worked on her drawing even later into the night. Once up on Sunday, she spent her free time signing and addressing Christmas cards.

Nick admired her sketch of their house. "It's all decked out for Christmas. Won't it look amazing a few years from now when we have that many lights?"

He liked the lights she'd drawn. She'd have to get some, no, *lots* of lights. Even last minute sale prices wouldn't allow her to buy as many as she'd drawn. Her mom had plenty of extra lights, but shipping would be a small fortune. She pondered what happened to castoff lights, and the solution presented itself. She'd scour the thrift stores before she went to work at eleven tomorrow.

The next evening, she hauled three overstuffed grocery bags into the house after work. Nick met her in the foyer. "What on earth have you got there?"

"Lights. The Humane Society Thrift Store had them on special—today only. All you can stuff in a bag for a dollar."

His grin was the only thanks she could ever want.

She smiled back at him. "I thought you could put them up on Saturday. We don't have to wait years to make the house look amazing. We can do it now."

He shook his head. "You're what's amazing. I never would have thought to buy used lights."

She shrugged off his compliment. "I plugged them all in at the store. They work, but some of the strings are a bit tangled."

He hugged her, bags and all, then held up a snarl of lights. "My dad *told* me to major in engineering."

"Mine would have been happy if I'd taken *anything* but art."

Nick pointed at the dining room table. "Speaking of your dad, a box came for you from your folks."

"Really? What could it be? Mom said their gift to us would come from Amazon."

She hurried to the table and ripped the tape off the box. Soon the flaps lay open, and Whitney picked a letter off the top. "Mom wanted us to feel at home, so she sent my stocking along with all the ornaments I made through the years and..." She grinned as she lifted the one new item from the box. "...some lights for the tree!"

They laughed together as Whitney unloaded the treasures of her childhood. She set the stocking aside, wondering if she could get Nick's from his mom in time. She'd call her mother-in-law when Nick wasn't home. Taking a wad of tissue paper from the box, she unwrapped it. "Oh, I remember this one. It took forever to glue all those Popsicle sticks together."

Nick admired each ornament, never commenting on their shabbiness, but Whitney couldn't help but think of the gorgeous decorations on his mother's tree last year. "I'm going to make a wreath like the one in my drawing and decorate it with these."

"But what will we put on our tree?" Nick looked like someone had stolen Christmas.

She couldn't match the stylized splendor his mother had managed, but anything would be better than this dog-eared mess. She sifted through the pile again. "I know." She lifted up her old Raggedy Ann doll her mother had included in the box. "The thrift store's dollar-a-bag item tomorrow is stuffed animals. I can get enough little ones to fill our tree for a couple of bucks."

Nick took her face in his hands and kissed her long and sweet. "Smart and beautiful, too. How'd I get so lucky?"

At Whit's End ~ 5

IT TOOK OVER an hour after work the next day to pick out the stuffed animals. Most were in decent shape, but only the best would do for their tree, and they had to be small. When she had three plastic bags bulging full, she wandered past the Christmas decorations and grabbed twenty feet of garland for only a quarter. That should add some sparkle.

She only worked mornings on Tuesdays, so she'd be able to work on the sketch before she had to make dinner. The manager at the craft store had sold her two eleven-by-fourteen inch frames, three five-by-seven frames, and a dented piece of matting for less than half price. She hadn't needed the three smaller frames, but the set was inventoried that way, so he couldn't break it up. With her discount, both presents would only cost twenty-five dollars. If she got them done this week, she wouldn't have to pay express shipping, so she'd have at least fifty dollars to add to Nick's present. That would cover Santa's visit.

A glimmer of regret over shorting their parents raised its ugly head, but she squelched it. If she'd paid full price for the frames and matting, let alone the usual price for custom framing, the gifts would have cost well over their budgeted amount. That didn't even count what an artist would charge to sketch the houses. *I am an artist*, she reminded herself. Her work was every bit as good as anyone she could have hired. Still, her father's voice nagged at her, telling her art was a hobby, not a profession.

To prove him wrong, she spent a little extra time shading her sketch. Her mother's camellia bush came alive, and light all but glinted off the windows. It was a very good likeness of her childhood home, if she did say so herself.

The sound of the front door startled her. Nick was home. How could it be that late? She gathered her supplies and stashed them in her portfolio. "Hey, I'll be right there," she called to him. What could she serve for dinner? How could she explain what she'd been doing?

She found her husband at the dining room table, poking through the bags of stuffed animals, an expectant look on his face. He turned toward her. "There you are."

"Hi. Dinner's not in there." She laughed to buy herself some time. "I thought we'd, uh, have soup and sandwiches tonight." She tried to sound like she thought that was a perfectly acceptable dinner, but she knew better. After all, she only worked part-time, and his job required extra hours. She should have made a decent meal before working on her sketch.

"Sounds great. One of our clients sent a huge tin of Christmas cookies to the office today, so a light dinner is perfect. If you don't need help cooking, I'll change while you get it ready."

"That's fine." Whew. That was a close one. She'd better plan dinners ahead from now on. She put some chicken noodle soup in the microwave and used Thanksgiving leftovers to make thick sandwiches. At least she had a pumpkin pie in the freezer. She could give Nick one of his favorite desserts.

When it came time for the pie, Whitney decided it was also time to broach the subject she'd been pondering ever since the thrift store that afternoon. "I got lots of good stuffed animals for the tree, but there's one problem."

"What's that?"

She tried to sound casual. "We don't have a tree." She waited for a moment to let him digest the dilemma. "I thought we might be able to get a small one at the stand down the street. If we get it now, we'll have it in the house longer, so it's a better value."

Nick stared into space so long, she wondered if he'd heard her. Finally, he cleared his throat. "I'd forgotten trees cost money. We used to go cut our own on my grandpa's land."

He'd never mentioned that. "I'm sure we could find a cut-your-own place not far away. This area is full of trees. After all, Washington's the Evergreen State."

Nick took out his phone and tapped on the screen. "There are several tree farms nearby, but I don't think we can get anything for the nineteen dollars we have left for decorating."

"Nineteen?" She remembered him saying twenty-five. Oh, the six dollars she'd spent at the thrift store for lights and toys made the difference. Her mind sought for a solution. They had to have a tree. "Make the tree my Christmas present. You haven't bought anything yet, right?"

"No, but I wanted to get you something special—something you'd have for a long time, not a tree that will go out in the trash the week after Christmas." His mouth drooped, and lines appeared at the corners of his eyes.

"Let's at least go look on Saturday after I get off work. Maybe we'll find a Charlie Brown tree that doesn't cost much."

Saturday afternoon brought the typical heavy winter rain interrupted occasionally by lighter rain. During one light spell, they drove five miles out of town to Henrich's Tree Farm. It didn't take long to discover that even a three-foot tree cost more than they had allotted. With the fifty dollars set aside for Nick to buy a present for his wife, they could afford a beautiful seven-foot noble fir, but Nick found something wrong with each one.

Finally, when they'd circumnavigated back to the cashier stand, Whitney couldn't take it. "What's wrong? You don't like any of them."

"What am I supposed to do on Christmas morning? Throw a blanket over the tree, so you can unwrap your present? Why don't we see if we can buy a fake tree on sale? It would last for years. Then I could still buy you a present. I haven't bought anything yet, but I have something in mind that will take the whole amount."

"That does make good financial sense, but fake trees don't smell good like real trees."

Nick kicked at the dirt and stuffed his hands in his pocket, a sure sign his stubborn side was about to make an appearance. "There's got to be a way to compromise." He looked around as if the answer grew on the trees. "Look." He pointed at the area where purchases were trimmed for loading onto cars and minivans. "See that pile of branches?"

Without waiting for her response, he marched over to the attendant. "Could we have some of those branches? My wife wants to make a wreath and decorate with them."

The young man looked at the jumble of evergreen castoffs and shrugged. "Sure. We have to burn them if no one takes them."

Nick piled the greens in the trunk of their car. "This is great! The house will smell good, and a fake tree will be easy to put up and take down."

"Yeah." She couldn't muster any more enthusiasm. Of course he was right. He'd hit on a good compromise, but he hadn't even asked how she felt about it. Her side of the car remained quiet on the ride to the department store. Nick babbled on about some big project he was working on for a major client. She tried to grunt at the appropriate times, but she kept thinking about the beautiful tree she'd drawn on her Christmas cards. No fake piece of plastic could ever compare.

One look at the sign in front of the store clinched it. "Artificial Trees 60% Off!" Great. Nick would find one he liked within their budget, and she'd have to go along with it no matter what it looked like.

Nick marched right to the seasonal aisle, and Whitney followed, shuffling her feet. Of course they'd have the stupid things all decorated with twinkling lights and the most expensive ornaments.

Each tree had a stack of cards in front of it. You evidently took the card to the counter, and a stocker brought the tree from the back. They had circled the display almost back to the front when Nick stopped. "There it is—the tree in your picture."

It did look like her tree. Maybe this wouldn't be so bad, but forty percent of the original price still topped their allotment by ten dollars. Nick turned the price tag over on the smaller tree next to it.

Naturally, it fell within their budget. She couldn't think of anything to say to convince him to reject it. All she could do was snort at the lower price.

Nick looked at her with a strange, almost pained expression. Then his face crunched itself up into the look of concentration she'd always loved.

The longer he thought, the more she wanted this tree. It wasn't what she'd wanted when they left home, but it was close enough. The cheaper one next to it looked shabby and small in comparison. She considered trying to influence him but decided to wait patiently for him to work it out.

Nick studied both trees, glaring at each of the price tags again. "It's only ten dollars, but we're on a tight budget until I get my raise and benefits. Then we won't have to worry about saving for medical and dental bills. The mortgage is more than I'd planned for housing. We really can't stretch it any further."

She could almost hear his thoughts. She'd been the one who wanted the house. They couldn't have the house and the perfect tree, too. She reached out to take a card for the smaller tree. If they set it up on top of the end table, it would look bigger from the outside. They could always get a bigger tree, maybe a real one, next year.

Nick suddenly straightened and grabbed her arm, directing it to the cards in front of the larger tree. "I've got it. We can cancel the newspaper for December. That's enough to pay the extra. What do you think?"

All the resentment she'd let build up melted away. "You love to read the sport section. That's not fair to you."

"It's only for a month, and there's an online edition that has most of what I read, anyway. Let's do it."

She threw her arms around her husband. "Thank you."

He gave her a quick peck on the forehead, never one for public displays of affection. "Merry Christmas."

More than ever, she determined to do everything she could to make this Christmas all he could wish for. They'd decorate the tree tomorrow, and Christmas would officially begin.

As they reached the line for the cashier, Nick pointed to a display of gift cards. "Have you mailed our parents' Christmas cards yet? We could put a gift card right in the envelope."

Maybe the time had come to tell him about her sketches. No, she wanted to show them to him finished and framed. "I haven't sent their cards because I'm going to include them in their gifts. I've already started something, but I don't want to tell you yet. I'll be ready in a couple of days."

He shot her a questioning look. "Is this why you've been getting up at night? What are you up to?"

Oh, no! He knew she hadn't been sleeping much. "You just wait and see."

Cocking his head, he peered at her, a worried look on his face. "Don't wear yourself out. There are lots of Christmases to come."

She didn't care about the future. She wanted to make this first year alone together magical for her husband, but Nick didn't seem to think she could do it. An ache pinched inside her. The rows of Christmas decorations surrounding them mocked her homemade attempts.

On the ride home, she began to second guess her decision. Maybe she should have gone with gift cards, so she could spend more time doing things for Nick. However, pleasing his parents would please him, too; wouldn't it? Her father's doubts about her art crept into her mind. What if Nick didn't think the picture good enough for his parents?

She couldn't worry about that. She'd better concentrate on getting it done. If she didn't mail the gifts by Friday, standard postage wouldn't get them there in time.

At Whit's End ~ 6

AFTER CHURCH ON Sunday, Nick wanted to drive to Snoqualmie Falls. "We haven't seen much of the area, and it's a nice day today. It's not supposed to rain until late in the afternoon."

Whitney had hoped to get a couple of hours in on the picture of her in-laws' house while Nick watched football. "Isn't there a game today?"

"I don't care. I'd rather spend time with you. I'm going to have to work late this week, and today is our only whole day together. Everyone at work says the falls are spectacular, especially this time of year when the river is high. The hike to the bottom isn't too long, and it's a beautiful drive out there."

When she hesitated, he added, "You seem so tired lately. I think the fresh air would do us both good."

She evidently didn't succeed in keeping the sourness she felt off her face because he shrugged and said, "If you don't want to go, we won't."

She forced a smile. "Of course I want to go with you. It surprised me, is all." She got her jacket and headed for the front door even though the undone work in her studio pulled at her. She'd have to work later into the night than usual—if she could stay awake.

After an awe inspiring drive through towering forests and steep mountainsides, they stood at the observation deck and admired the thundering falls. The stress and worry of the season washed away in the spray that reached out to them. Whitney squeezed Nick's hand. "I'm so glad we came."

He put his arm around her shoulders and held her tightly for several moments. "I can feel the energy from the falls vibrating in every cell of my body. It goes right through me."

"It *is* overpowering. Isn't it?"

He glanced over at her with a sly smile and raised an eyebrow. "It's the way I felt when I realized I wanted to marry you."

She gave him a playful slap. "It seems I married the only romantic accountant on the planet."

"Oh, no, we accountants are a very romantic lot. We never get credit for it, but it's one of our greatest assets. Let me show you." He swept her into an embrace and covered her face in kisses.

They climbed down some stairs, holding hands, and looked out at the falls from a lower perspective.

Tall evergreens marched along the rocky cliffs, providing a patchwork of grey and green.

Nick pointed at a sign marking the path to the bottom of the falls. "The map out front showed a parking lot at the bottom." They looked down the dirt track glistening from the recent rains. He shook his head. "Let's go back up and drive down to that lot. I don't want either of us to fall and break a leg. Our insurance isn't in effect yet."

They clambered up the stairs and drove to the lower lot. A boardwalk set among the towering firs led from the powerhouse to the bottom of the falls. The water cascaded into a pool, churning and frothing at the bottom. Whitney's breath caught. "Oh, I feel like the water's pulling me down with it."

Nick put his arms around her and lifted her off her feet. "I'll hold you up."

She laughed. "Put me down, you clown."

He turned her around to face him. "I mean it. I'll never let you fall, Whit. Never."

She snuggled up against him. "I'm going to hold you to that."

They hiked around for a while then headed back home. It seemed a long time since they'd spent a day together, and Whitney wished it didn't have to end.

It wasn't until the sinking sun reminded her that the day would, indeed, soon end that Whitney thought about her Christmas preparations. Even if she lost extra sleep making up the time, the day enjoying the woods and water had been worth it.

At Whit's End ~ 7

THE WEEK FLEW by with Whitney working on the sketches whenever Nick was at work or asleep and assembling the wreath when they were both home, which wasn't often. The craft store kept running last minute specials and coupon extravaganzas, so all the employees were given extra hours. The money would be nice when it finally showed up in January, but she needed the time now to get everything ready.

On Wednesday evening, she heard the front door open a little earlier than she'd expected. She swept the sketch of his parents' house out of sight and scooted over to the table where her half-finished wreath waited. She grabbed the pliers and twisted wire around a fir twig, holding it in place. She picked up another and started to attach it as Nick poked his head into the room.

"Hey. Have you eaten yet?"

"No." She wanted to snap that she'd been working on his parents' present, and now he'd come home early, and she couldn't get any more done. Instead, she hurried to twist the wire into place and caught part of her finger in the process. "Ow!"

Nick rushed to her. "What happened?"

"I pinched myself." It came out irritated, accusing.

Nick took her hand, turning it, so he could see the wound. "That looks nasty. You're working too fast."

"Maybe if I didn't have so much to do, I wouldn't have to hurry."

"You don't have to make a wreath."

"Yes, I do. I don't have enough money to buy a fake one, and we got the branches from the tree farm, so I have to make it."

"I meant it's okay if we don't have a wreath this year. It's too much work."

Of course they had to have a wreath. His mother always had a wreath. Besides, her childhood ornaments sat in the box from home, waiting to decorate it. They had to have a wreath or... She didn't finish the thought. Tears welled up and overcame her ability to think or talk. She swallowed down the lump in her throat and blinked back the tears. Didn't he think she, an artist, couldn't make a wreath? "Your dinner's in the oven. I'm not eating."

"Whit, come on. What's wrong?"

"Nothing. I want to finish this, and I'm not hungry. Go eat." She kept her voice steady, but he didn't seem appeased.

"Really, what's wrong? Is it my long hours? That will be over this week, and I'll be home more."

She spat the words at him. "It's not about you."

His shoulders tightened, making his suit pull up around them. His mouth puckered for a moment. Then he took a deep breath and let it out. He obviously chose his words carefully. "You're pushing yourself too much. You aren't sleeping enough, and now you won't eat dinner."

"I have too much to do. There's baking to do and this wreath to finish, and the lights aren't up on the house."

"Then it does come back to me. I'm sorry I haven't gotten that done. This project at work—"

"I know. It's *so* important." It *was* important. He'd explained it a hundred times. Something inside her deflated, leaving her worn out. "I mean I know it's important. I'm just tired."

Nick's shoulders relaxed. He looked at her as if she were sick and adopted a soothing tone. "I'll hang the lights on Saturday. I promise, no matter what the weather's like. I know how much you want this Christmas to be special."

"I want it special for you." She knew it sounded argumentative, so she softened her voice. "Come on, I'll eat with you. The wreath can wait."

At Whit's End ~ 8

FRIDAY MORNING DAWNED to find Whitney in her studio putting the finishing touches on the drawing of her in-laws' home. She'd sketched until midnight, but after a few hours of fitful catnaps, she'd gotten up and gone back to work.

Now, she attached the newly finished sketch to the back of the matting she'd prepared and slipped it into the frame as Nick came down the stairs. By the time he entered the room, both sketches were displayed on a shelf.

Whitney stood back. "What do you think?"

Nick stared without speaking, and Whitney held her breath. Finally, he turned to her with his lips pressed together. "Oh, Whit, it's... beautiful." His voice choked, and he turned back to the picture of his childhood home. "Look, there's my tire swing." He pointed to a window. "And the light's on in my room." He pulled his wife to him. "My parents will love this. It's so much better than a gift card. When did you find the time?"

"I couldn't sleep thinking of all I wanted to do for Christmas."

"Do you have money left for shipping? Those frames must have cost the whole budget."

"Uh, I have enough left for postage. I get a discount at the store; you know." She hadn't lied, but Whitney felt a twinge of guilt. She'd explain after Christmas, after Santa came, and she could tell him what she'd done with the extra money.

Nick hugged her again and went back to admiring the pictures. "Oh, I know I promised to hang the lights tomorrow, and I will, but I have to work in the morning. The deadline for my project is coming up, and I *have* to have it done. The client needs the cost analysis for expansion before his end-of-year report to his shareholders."

Her spirits sank. "There's only two more weeks until Christmas. All the neighbors have their lights up."

"I'll do everything I can to get home in time to do it." He studied her face. "This is a very substantial account. It has to be done by next Friday, and it has to be done right. My raise depends on it."

He worried so much about finances. They had some money left in the bank, but he refused to spend it. "It's for a rainy day," he'd say whenever she suggested they could tap into what they'd saved for recreation or Christmas. She'd laugh and say, "This is Seattle. It rains every day."

On Saturday morning, Whitney easily finished the wreath and hung it on the door. Since she wasn't scheduled to work, she busied herself with baking and tried not to look out the window at the neighbor's lights and yard decorations. Whenever her eyes disobeyed and slipped to the window, her thoughts traveled to Nick and how he hadn't done the one thing she'd asked him to do to help get ready for Christmas. She mentally chided herself, remembering that he had to work, how important this project was to him, and he'd promised to do it when he got home. But the cycle repeated every time she spied her neighbor's copious strings of lights.

They'd met the Yeagers across the street when they first moved in, but they hadn't really talked until Tim Yeager, a rambunctious ten year old, crashed his bike into the rhododendron out front a few days ago. Whitney had rushed out to help the boy, but his mother came running at the same time, scolding her son for his speed and recklessness. When Tim jumped on his bike and raced away, Mrs. Yeager thanked Whitney for her help. "They say it takes a village to raise a child. With that one, it might take the whole city."

Maybe Whitney should take some of the goodies she made across the street to Tim and his family. She put the thought aside. Surely, Mrs. Yeager made her own special treats each year. Besides, there seemed to be a whole herd of children over there. It would take a platter full of sweets to make a dent in their appetites. She put it off to think of later and popped a tray of cookies in the oven.

By four o'clock, she'd baked Russian tea cakes, sugar cookies, and fruit cake and made two batches of fudge. The dishes were done, and dinner was in the oven. The last few Christmas cards had been sent. She still needed to pick up a few things for Nick's stocking and shop for the special Christmas dinner she had planned, but she wanted to be home when Nick got there, so that could wait.

The sound of a car drew her eyes to the window. It wasn't Nick, but in the dimming afternoon light, it seemed that every neighbor had turned on their Christmas lights, and the whole street twinkled at her.

That did it.

She grabbed a bag of lights and headed outside. She could string them around the door and windows. She'd have to use the ladder, but she wouldn't have to go up it very far. Then Nick would only have to do the roofline when he had time. She punched the code into the garage door opener and tried to remember where Nick stored the ladder.

She started at the door and made a circular sweep of the walls. The ladder leaned against the far wall next to a pile of scrap lumber the previous owners had left. She got it and dragged it to the front step. Twisting and turning it one way and then another, she finally arranged it safely in front of the door. She took a deep breath and climbed two steps to gaze at the top of the door frame. Her breath escaped in a rush when she found nails already embedded at strategic locations. There'd been lights here before. She only had to hook the strings of lights on the nails. She looked across the front of the house and found the windows similarly prepared. Encircling the door only took a few minutes, and she soon stood on the ground, ready to move on.

She dragged the ladder into the flower bed in front of the first window. She stepped up onto the ladder, but the front feet sank into the damp earth. She gasped, grabbed onto the window frame, and gingerly climbed back down.

Safely on the ground, she went back to the garage and retrieved a piece of plywood from the scrap pile. Laying the wood on the ground, she placed the ladder on it, put one foot on the first rung, and pressed lightly. The ladder didn't tip, so she pushed a little harder. It still held, and she put her weight on the step and climbed higher. With that problem solved, she strung the lights around both windows.

She stood back to admire her work. It wasn't all she'd imagined, but it was a start, and if Nick got the rest of the lights up, it would be close enough. At least theirs wouldn't be the only dark house on the street once she turned them on. How could she have forgotten? She had no idea how to get power to the lights.

The plugs hung down from each string, waiting to be inserted into outlets, but there were no outlets nearby any of them. After hanging them herself, the helplessness of not knowing how to make it all work pinched her throat, and the first tears formed at the corners of her eyes.

How stupid. It couldn't be that hard.

She gazed at the house next door. Her eyes traveled down the string of lights around their front window to an orange extension cord tucked into the groove in the siding and along the ground to an outside receptacle. Of course, extension cords.

She ran to the garage and made a hasty search of Nick's work bench. She scanned the wall and found two extension cords hanging from nails.

Back outside, she found an outlet near the door. A quick examination of the extension cords revealed each had three places to plug cords into. The lights around the windows would both plug into one of the cords if she took down one of the strings and wound it around the window in the opposite direction. That done, she plugged both strings of lights into the cord and ran it along the foundation to the outlet but didn't plug it in. She had to wind the lights around the door in the opposite direction, too. Now, it would reach the outlet without an extension cord.

She plugged in the window lights. Nothing. She plugged in the door lights. Nothing. Now what?

At that moment, Nick's car pulled into the driveway. She glanced at her watch. She'd spent an hour putting up the lights, so he wouldn't have so much to do, and now they didn't work. Her shoulders sagged. She blew out her breath and put on a smile to greet her husband. "Hey, you're finally home."

"Sorry. There was a little snag, but we got it worked out." He came toward her, looking tired, then seemed to brighten. "Wow. You put up the lights."

"Only the ones I could reach." She scrunched her face up and bit back the tears she felt forming again. "But they don't turn on."

"Did you flip the switch in the entry?"

"Switch?"

"Yeah. That outlet is switched from inside."

"Why did they do that?"

He laughed. "For Christmas lights. You don't have to come out in the rainy dark to plug and unplug them. You flip the switch from inside."

Whitney stepped inside and flipped the switch she'd never noticed. A myriad of twinkling colors erupted, lighting up her husband's face. She felt herself light up every bit as much. "How wonderful!"

Nick smiled up at her. "I'm so glad you were able to do that. I'm beat. You'd think sitting at a desk all day wouldn't be tiring, but it is. I dreaded putting up the lights all the way home."

Obviously, she couldn't ask him to climb to the top of the ladder and put lights on the roof lines now. Besides, it was getting dark. Maybe he could do it tomorrow after church.

The winter storm that blew in over Saturday night lasted for three days. Freezing, slanted rain pelted down relentlessly. Deb at work sang, "I'm dreaming of a wet Christmas," over and over until it wasn't funny anymore. Nick couldn't possibly put the lights up, but they got the tree centered in front of the window and spent the evenings arranging and rearranging the stuffed animals on its branches until they both pronounced it perfect.

Whitney wound the garland around the tree, remembering how her father always glumped tinsel on the branches. Her mother had finally banned him from helping with that part. Oh, after all these years, it suddenly became obvious that her father had planned that very outcome.

At Whit's End ~ 9

THE RAIN FINALLY slacked off, but the cold continued on. Between the weather and the long hours Nick spent at work finishing his project, the lights remained in their bag, and the roof remained dark. Whitney looked down the street at the twinkling rooflines of her neighbors and forced herself to be satisfied with the lights she'd managed to hang herself—until Saturday.

She awoke to the familiar sound of rain hitting the window. Oh, no. With Christmas Eve only a few days away, the rest of the lights weren't up. Nick groaned in his sleep and rolled over. He'd worked even later than usual last night, but he'd completed the project. His boss had slapped him on the back and told him to look forward to his four month review in

February. Then he'd get a raise, and they could relax the budget. Their worries would be over.

Really, in the great scheme of the universe, it didn't matter that their house had only half as many lights as she'd sketched on their Christmas cards. She'd let him sleep and make pancakes for breakfast. She pulled back the covers to slip out of bed as Nick's cell phone jangled on his nightstand.

She hurried around the bed to get it before he woke, but he reached out and grabbed it. "Hello. Oh, hi, Mom." He sat up and shrugged at his wife. "You got it already? Great." He gave Whitney a thumbs-up and grinned. His parents must like the picture. "She *is* a great artist. That sketch is going to be worth a lot of money someday."

Whitney rolled her eyes at her husband and sat on the bed next to him. He put the phone on speaker, so she could hear her mother-in-law. "And the drawing of your new house on the card is wonderful, too. You've got to take a picture of it now that it's decorated for Christmas. Whitney can use the comparison in her portfolio."

Nick nodded even though his mother couldn't see him. "I'll do that. I'm glad you like the picture."

"Tell Whitney the package should arrive today, and don't ask any questions about it."

"Okay." He punched end on his phone and gave his wife a quizzical look but kept his promise to his mother. "They love it, of course. It's going above the mantle in the living room."

It had all been worth it. "I'm so glad."

The sound of rain pelting the window reminded her. "You can go back to sleep if you want. I'm making pancakes, and you don't have to hang the lights. What we have is enough."

"No. I'll eat pancakes, but I promised." He took her hand. "I'll always keep my promises to you. The rain is supposed to stop by noon. I'll be on the ladder a minute later."

Her willingness to sacrifice having more lights paled in comparison to his desire to keep his promise to her. She threw herself at him, wrapping her arms around him and pushing him back down on the bed.

An hour later, she rinsed the last of the sticky syrup off their plates as she thought through the last minute details. Nick's stocking should arrive from his mother that afternoon. Now she could buy a tangerine, nuts, and candy to add to the little gifts she had hidden away. She needed to call Santa and confirm the time of his visit, but that would have to wait until Nick wasn't around. Today, she wanted to make gifts for her coworkers.

Since her Christmas budget was depleted, she'd decided to make sketches of each of the three gals in her department. She'd used her cell phone to take snapshots of their employee pictures in the break room. The quality wasn't great, but she knew these ladies, so that should help. She had the smaller frames left over, so it wouldn't cost her anything but time. She told Nick her plan and retreated to her studio while he watched the UW Huskies play in the warmth of the Arizona sun.

She worked quickly, aided by the pictures and her knowledge of the women, and she had made good progress on the second sketch when she heard Nick yell, "We won," from the other room.

She closed her sketchpad and put the supplies she'd been using in her pencil case. By the time she reached the living room, Nick had left. She migrated to the dining room. He wasn't there, and neither were the lights. He hadn't forgotten his promise. She poked her head out the front door in time to see him exit the garage with the ladder.

As thrilled as she was to think he was finally going to hang the upper lights, a twinge of guilt nagged at her. "You don't *have* to do that. You've been working so hard. I know you'd rather rest."

"Nonsense. The rain stopped during the last quarter. It's almost noon, and I promised to be on this ladder at one after. Besides, the gutters are a little clogged. I can clean them out while I'm up there."

His sensible approach took a little of the joy out of finally getting the lights up, but she wouldn't let that ruin it. "I'll make a warm lunch for when you're done. How does chili sound?"

"Great. This shouldn't take more than an hour."

"I'll be ready." She pulled her head back inside but stepped out on the porch a second later and pointed at the flower bed under the window. "Be careful. That dirt is soft. I had to put a board down before I could climb the ladder."

"Good idea. I'll get one."

Satisfied that he was all set for the job, she went

back inside. Cornbread would go great with chili, and she had plenty of time, so she went to the kitchen. As she worked on the recipe, her mind worked on organizing the next few days. She should be able to finish the portraits in time to take them to work with her on Tuesday morning. She could leave them in the women's cubbies in the break room, so they'd be there when the ladies came to work.

She popped the cornbread into the oven and opened the cupboard door to find the chili. A shadow blocked the light, and she turned to see that Nick had the ladder in front of the kitchen window. Gluck from the gutter splattered Nick's leg followed by a gush of water. He'd probably want a shower before lunch.

Whitney turned back to the cupboard but stopped when light poured back into the room. She turned back to the window in time to see the foot of the ladder fly past. Staring toward the window, she wondering what had happened until Nick's frantic voice called her name. She flew out the front door.

The flower bed looked like it had been plowed. The ladder sprawled across the lawn, and Nick lay on the sidewalk, one leg twisted under the other at an odd angle. She ran to him. "What happened?"

"I fell." Even deadpanning the joke, pain edged his voice.

"Can you move?"

"Not sure." His face contorted as he shifted slightly. "Awwww." When he relaxed a little, he whispered, "Nope."

"I'm calling for an ambulance."

"Yep."

She ran into the house. Nick had resisted all her attempts to get him to the doctor when he'd thrown up for three days last year. If he wanted an ambulance, it was bad. She raced through the house, unable to remember where she'd left her phone. On her second pass through the dining room, she made herself stop and think. Nick's phone still lay on his bedside table. She raced down the hall and grabbed it, dialing 9-1-1 as she came back down the hall.

By the time the operator answered, Whitney knelt next to Nick. "My husband fell off a ladder. I think his leg is broken."

"Has he tried to move?"

"Yes. He can't." She gazed at his wrinkled brow. "He's in a lot of pain."

"I'm sending the ambulance." She confirmed their address and said, "Stay on the line."

Whitney sank further into the wet grass. "They're coming, sweetie. Hang in there."

He nodded his head slightly, obviously not wanting to cause another jolt of pain. Whitney gently patted his head and answered the operator's questions concerning Nick's name, age, and general physical condition.

Nick stared up at her, eyes wide and mouth compressed. She murmured reassurances to him, all the while hoping her words were true. What if he couldn't work? They had to make their house payments. Why, oh why, had she made such a fuss about the lights? She never would have if she'd known what it would cost. Cost! The ambulance, the hospital, the doctor would each take more and more money. With no insurance, they'd have to pay it all. They could lose the house.

Nick looked even more pained, but his voice sounded stronger when he spoke. "Don't worry. It's not that bad."

"I know. They'll fix you right up." Better not to tell him her worries went beyond his immediate pain. He'd figure out they were in financial trouble soon enough.

The wail of the siren broke in, and she jumped up to wave her arms at the paramedics. The ambulance pulled to a stop in their driveway, and a middle-aged, graying man and a young woman with dark hair pulled into a pony tail jumped out.

The man hurried to Nick's side. The woman opened the back doors of the ambulance then watched her partner, who took one look at Nick's leg and waved to her. She pulled a gurney out and rolled it toward them.

The older EMT shifted, so he could talk to both Whitney and Nick. "It doesn't look good. It's going to hurt when we get him on the stretcher, so I want to start an IV drip of morphine. Any allergies?"

Nick shook his head no. Whitney bit her knuckle in an attempt to hold back the scream she felt rising in her throat. She had to be strong for Nick, let him concentrate on doing whatever he could to lessen the pain without worrying about her.

Salt-and-Pepper nodded toward his patient. "Talk to him."

Whitney knelt on Nick's other side and gently stroked his hand, careful not to bump his leg. "Remember how we drove down to the parking lot at the falls, so we wouldn't fall and break our legs?" She paused while he smiled. "Fat lot of good that did us, huh?" She kept her voice light, but her heart weighed on her. "I guess it's better to have it happen here than way out there."

The paramedics positioned themselves for the lift, and Whitney did her best to stay close to Nick but out of their way. At first, she could only think of how guilty she felt. It didn't seem the best subject to bring up right then, so she babbled about how Nick used to brag that he'd never broken a bone.

Nick winced when the man straightened his leg, and she talked faster. "When you do something, you do it up big. I'll give you that." The sound Nick made was part laugh, part groan. The look of pain on his face tore at Whitney's heart, and she didn't think she could talk anymore.

Pony Tail whispered, "Keep talking. Distract him."

What could she say? She launched on all the home improvement projects they could do in the spring, not mentioning they might not be there. "Maybe we could plant an apple tree in the backyard. When it's big, we'll have fruit, and our kids can put a tire swing in it like you had. And we should definitely pour cement in that flower bed."

As the EMTs lifted him onto the gurney, Nick's scream covered several octaves. The sound stabbed Whitney and echoed over and over in her mind, accompanying the thought, *You did this to him. You did this to him.*

At Whit's End ~ *10*

WHITNEY FOLLOWED THE stretcher to the back of the ambulance. Pony Tail helped push it into the opening and then turned to Whitney. "If you ride with us, you won't have a car there. Is there someone who could pick you up?"

The miles stretched between her and her parents. She could call someone from work, but she didn't feel close enough to any of them to ask a favor. "No. I guess I'd better drive myself."

Salt-and-Pepper closed the doors on Nick. "You might want to grab something to do. I'm pretty sure he's going to need surgery. You'll have a wait."

After making sure she knew how to get to the Emergency Room, they drove off, leaving her standing alone in the driveway.

It seemed forever, but the ambulance hadn't yet turned the corner when she did an about face and headed inside to get her keys and "something to do." The stupid string of Christmas lights hung from the fascia board like a snake dangling from a tropical tree, ready to strike.

She wanted to grab it and rip it down, but that would take time. She had to get to the hospital. She scooped her keys up from the entry table and looked around for something to take along. Of course, she'd take the sketches she'd been working on. She went to her studio and shoved her sketch book and pencil box into a canvas shopping bag. Then she turned off the oven on the gooey cornbread.

Twenty minutes later, she rushed into the ER only to be told to take a seat. The receptionist would let her know when she could "go back."

She eyed the canvas bag but couldn't focus enough to draw. She passed over the home improvement magazines and flipped through an old copy of *People*. Nothing held her attention. Nick lay behind that wall somewhere in pain because of her, because she cared more about getting ready for Christmas than she did about him.

What kind of person was she?

No, she'd done everything to make the holiday special for him. He wanted the goodies, Santa, all of it. She reached for another magazine to keep from examining her motives any further. The page she landed on showed a chocolate chip ad featuring a glittering house, all decorated for Christmas with a family making cookies in the window. See, that's what she had been trying to give Nick. She'd done it all for Nick; hadn't she?

The receptionist's voice saved her from answering. "Mrs. Saunders?"

Evidently, it wasn't the first time she'd said it. They'd only been married a year and a half, and not many people called her that. "Yes. Can I see my husband now?"

"Go through the doors to the right. A nurse will meet you there."

Whitney obeyed and then followed a brightly clad nurse down a hallway. Thoughts of what all this would cost crept into her mind. *Concentrate*, she told herself. Nothing matters but Nick.

The nurse pointed to an open doorway. "We're prepping him for surgery, but you can visit for a few minutes."

Whitney's throat tightened. What would she find inside? Was Nick pale and still or writhing in pain? She took a deep breath and peeked in.

"Hey." Nick raised a hand in greeting. "They said you were out there."

"Hi. Do you feel better?" She inched her way along the hospital bed to stand at his shoulder.

"Morphine is good stuff." His voice became a bit blurred. "They gave me something to put me to sleep, too. I can't believe I was so stupid...sloshed all that water onto the ladder. "

"No, it's my fault. I never should have nagged you about those lights." Her voice cracked, and the tears she'd been holding back streamed down he cheeks. "I'm so sorry."

"Don't cry. It wasn't the lights. I should have cleaned out the gutters before the rains got so bad. I'm not used to...this...Washington...weath..." His voice trailed off, and his eyelids drooped.

Another nurse patted Whitney on the shoulder. "It's time for his surgery. That's a nasty break. The doctor's going to have to clean it up and repair the damage. It could be a couple of hours. The orderly will take you to the surgery waiting room."

After half an hour and quick calls to both sets of parents, Whitney finally relaxed enough to get out her sketch book. She needed to get them done, and it would keep her mind off what was happening to Nick. Her own worry made it hard to give her coworker a happy expression, but she did her best to capture Deb's happy-go-lucky attitude.

She sketched and wandered to the doorway to look down the hall in turns. She didn't even know who would come to tell her how the surgery had gone, but checking made her feel that she was doing something.

An orderly finally appeared. Whitney jumped up but sank down again as he ushered in an older woman saying, "Your husband will be fine. It's a very routine procedure."

The grey haired woman nodded and took a seat. She picked up a magazine but didn't look at it. Instead, she addressed Whitney. "He's had this shunt replaced twice before. It's all part of his cancer treatment." She opened the magazine, still not looking at it. "It seems I live in waiting rooms."

The woman obviously wanted to talk. Whitney put her drawing aside. "I'm sorry. It must be very hard."

"Not really." The woman shook her head slowly as if remembering something. "Hearing the diagnosis was hard, and the hardest part is still to come, but this is just waiting. I can do that." She fanned the magazine absently. "Why are you here, dear?"

Whitney bit her lips for a moment. "My husband fell off a ladder and broke his leg. They have to operate." She nearly choked on the last word.

The woman handed her the box of tissue from the table between them. "I'm sure they'll fix him up right and proper."

Something in her soft voice and eyes broke through the last of Whitney's defenses, and the whole story broke out of her like wild horses from a corral. "So, you see, it's all my fault. I wanted so much to give him a special Christmas, and now he's hurt."

Even through her tears, Whitney noticed a twinkle in the older woman's eye. A knowing smile and a slight nod of her head made Whitney feel defensive. "You don't believe me."

"Of course I do. I've been in exactly your position. You were trying to give your husband what you thought he wanted."

"Yes, I...wait. Did you say, 'What I *thought* he wanted?'"

"We've all done it, dear." She finally put the magazine down. "When we were first married, I saved all my spending money for months to take Rick to a fancy dinner for his birthday. They had the most exquisite desserts." She laughed outright now. "I was thoroughly put out that he didn't seem to appreciate my sacrifice. It took three months and two arguments for him to finally say, 'Carol, I'd much rather have your wonderful meatloaf and a homemade birthday cake next year.' It's been his birthday feast ever since."

The woman leaned across the table. "You see, *I* wanted the fancy dinner and dessert. I figured he'd want what I wanted, so I sacrificed to give it to him." Settling back, she added, "It saves a lot of time and money to ask them what they want. I finally learned that."

Whitney collapsed against her chair. "Hmm." The truth she'd been squelching ever since she heard Nick fall blossomed. "He talked about all the things that made his childhood Christmases special, but I never asked him what he wants now."

The older woman patted her hand. "You are lucky to have a head start on something that took me years to figure out." The woman's eyes crinkled as she chuckled. "When I think of all the time we wasted on silly misunderstandings." Her eyes got misty, and she looked away.

Tears sprang to Whitney's eyes as well. She couldn't imagine knowing she would lose Nick. "Is there anything I can do for you?'

Carol wiped her eyes. "No, dear. We have everything we need. We have each other. She withdrew her hands and clasped them in her lap. "Rick's got enough time for us to make a few more memories. We leave on Monday for the cruise we've put off for years." She chuckled. "I get seasick, but it's what he's always wanted."

The longing in Carol's eyes communicated more than her words. Whitney stated the obvious. "You'll miss him a great deal."

"Yes, I will, but I would have missed not having him in my life even more. I've decided to quit worrying about the after and enjoy the time we have together. "

"I don't know if I could do that." Whitney thought of her carefree day at the falls with Nick. She wanted more days like that, but the mounting bills loomed in her mind. "I'm so worried about Nick and how we're going to pay for all this. How can I ignore that?"

"You can't change the circumstances, sweetie. You can only make the best of what comes along. Some of my most treasured memories are from when my plans fell completely apart."

At Whit's End ~ 11

A FEW MINUTES later, Whitney followed a nurse to the recovery room, a long hallway consisting of at least ten beds cordoned off by white sliding curtains. The nurse led her to one of the cubicles where Nick lay on a bed with his left leg in a cast and elevated. His face was slack, and his eyelids hung at half-mast.

She sat near him and held his hand. "How do you feel?"

"Hmmm." He raised his eyelids a bit and smiled slightly. "I think I need a nap." His eyes closed, and he started making the little sleeping noise she loved.

The nurse whispered, "He'll wake again soon. Nothing to worry about. The doctor will be here shortly."

Shortly turned out to be half an hour, but Nick woke for a few minutes a couple of times between periods of sleepiness. Finally, after twenty minutes, he seemed lucid enough to talk. Whitney apologized again.

Nick shifted in the bed but couldn't move much. "Really, it's not your fault. I pulled the guck from the gutter, and a ton of water followed it onto the ladder. When I stepped down, I slipped. I grabbed higher up on the ladder, and that made the whole thing go over sideways. "

Whitney couldn't let it go. "I wanted to make Christmas special for you, but now I wonder if I did it all for you or myself." She took a deep breath. "I never asked you what you wanted, so now I'm asking. What did *you* want for Christmas?"

He took her hand and kissed it. "Like we said, my only Christmas wish is to spend it with you. If that's in our house or at the hospital, that's all I need to make it the best holiday ever. Being with you is all I ever wanted."

The tears welled up again, and her nose started to sting. "I'm sorry. I thought I was doing it for you. I really did."

"I know. It's all right. We'll have a great Christmas yet. When I get out of here..."

A voice from outside their enclosure interrupted. "I'm afraid you're going to be spending Christmas upstairs in Room 205." A man in blue scrubs pulled back the curtain. "I'm Doctor Johnson. I performed the surgery on your leg. That was a pretty nasty break, and you are going to need to stay in the hospital where we can keep it completely immobile for at least four days. You might get to go home on Christmas afternoon if you are an exemplary patient."

"He will be," Whitney promised. "I want him home as soon as possible." She didn't mention that the mounting hospital costs weighed on her. The doctor didn't need to know that, and she didn't want to worry Nick with it now.

After the doctor left, Nick became serious. He took a deep breath. "I don't know how we're going to pay for all of this. I'm not sure exactly when my health insurance will kick in, but I don't think it's until next month."

"We'll figure something out. You need to concentrate on getting well. We aren't going to even talk about it again until you're better, and all the bills have come in." She leveled her most serious gaze at him. "Promise?"

He screwed up his mouth and stared back at her. Finally, he whispered, "I'll try."

After a while, Nick dozed off again. Whitney got out her sketchbook and tried to concentrate on getting Deb's nose right.

"That's lovely." Evidently, the nurse in the wild scrubs had slipped in without Whitney noticing.

"Thank you. It's my coworker's Christmas present. I just finished it." Whitney shifted the pad to let the nurse see.

"You're very talented."

Smiling her thanks, Whitney turned the page then brought up Trish's picture on her cell as the nurse checked Nick's vitals and made some notes. As she passed to go out, she paused next to Whitney. "You can draw that well from a picture?"

Whitney shrugged. "I majored in art." She quickly blocked in Trish's face shape and long, curly hair.

The multi-colored fabric of the scrubs stayed put so long, Whitney finally looked up. The nurse had a look of deep concentration and didn't respond at first. After a moment, she pursed her lips and nodded her head. "This may be a little unprofessional of me, but do you sell your work? I mean, could I commission you to draw my daughter?" She pulled a picture out of her pocket. "It's her sixteenth birthday in a couple of weeks, and it would be a wonderful present for her."

"Sure. We're going to be here a few days. I can bring back some pastel portraits to show you. Then you can choose pencil or color."

"That would be wonderful. What would a color portrait cost compared to black and white?"

"Actually, it's about the same amount of time and effort, so I charge..." She thought back to her college friend's pricelist. "...seventy-five dollars either way for up to an eleven by fourteen inch. If you want it bigger, or if you want me to frame it, I'd charge a little extra." She tried to sound confident and not like she was making up the prices as she went.

"Wonderful. I'm on shift again tomorrow afternoon. Your husband is going to be in 205, right?"

"Yes. I'll have some samples to show you then."

The nurse hurried out, and Whitney went back to work. Seventy-five dollars wouldn't pay even one of the medical bills, but turning her talent into cash might make a difference in the long run.

Over the next few hours, Nick roused completely, and two orderlies moved him to his new room on the second floor. When they had the patient situated comfortably for the night, he insisted his wife go home to sleep. "I'm fine. Nothing's going to happen here tonight except the nurses waking me up to see if I need a sleeping pill."

When she hesitated, he added, "Besides, I won't be alone. I need to call my folks and let them hear my voice. You go home, but come back as soon as you can in the morning." He looked around as if to make sure none of the staff could hear. "I hate these places."

She kissed him goodbye, determined to honor her mandate of not discussing their impending financial doom until they had the facts.

At Whit's End ~ 12

WHITNEY WOKE THE next morning and looked over to see if Nick had gotten up yet, but his side of the bed hadn't been slept in. Then it all flooded back—the fall, the ambulance, the hospital. The clock read not quite seven. She'd have plenty of time to gather some of her art and get to the hospital before eight.

Then it hit her. Santa...cookies in the freezer... a tree full of stuffed animals...all gone to waste. She'd call Santa later and cancel. She'd have to pay him, anyway. She knew that from the elf girl at the mall. They'd be eating Christmas goodies until Valentine's Day, but at least they'd have something to eat. They wouldn't be able to afford groceries.

On her way out the door, her phone rang, and she finally found it under the mail on the dining room table. Her mother's voice sounded worried. "How's Nick? Do you want me to come?"

"Thanks for offering, Mom, but there's no need. The doctor says he should heal completely."

"That's such a relief. Well, if you're sure everything's okay, your father wants to talk to you about something else."

Whitney waited while her parents traded places. Her heart thumped in her chest. If Dad wanted to talk, it must be serious. He usually only spoke a few words of greeting and gave the phone to her mother.

"Whit?"

"Yeah, Dad, it is everything okay?"

He didn't respond immediately, and she held her breath. Finally, her father cleared his throat. "I wanted to tell you I...I was wrong." He seemed to struggle for the right words. "About your art. The picture you did of our house is...well, it's amazing." Was he actually sniffing? "I spent so many years discouraging something I thought was frivolous. But that drawing of our house...Well, I'm glad you didn't listen to me about your major. You are a very talented girl."

"Oh, Dad, you don't know how much that means to me. I'm so glad you like it." She hung up, feeling restored and ready to face whatever the world wanted to throw at her.

When she got to Room 205, Nick sat up in bed, more or less. His left leg hung from a chain, but otherwise, he looked comfortable. He grinned at her. "Here's the medicine I need."

She went to him and kissed him. "I missed you when I woke."

"I'm glad you slept. You'd have thought I was giving out money in here the way people came and went through the night."

She smoothed his hair. "I'm sure it's all necessary, but I'm sorry you didn't get much sleep." She pulled a chair next to his bed and sat. "You sleep whenever you want today. Don't worry about me. I brought things to keep myself occupied." She pointed at her bag. "Actually, when I finish the pictures for the gals at work, I'll need to run over there to deliver them."

Nick's eyes grew wide. "You have a shift today. When do you need to be there?"

"I called Deb. She's going to cover it for me."

"Good." He pointed at the chain holding up his leg. "It'll be much easier to be tied up if you're here."

They talked for a while until Nick's eyes drooped, and his words came out mumbled. Whitney sat quietly for a few minutes, listening for the whiffle that meant he was asleep. When it came, she got out her sketch of Trish. It shouldn't take long to finish it with Trish's regular features.

After twenty minutes of sitting in the hard chair, Whitney decided she needed a short walk. She left her drawing on the chair to reassure Nick she'd be right back if he woke.

She wandered down the hall. The gift shop was closed, and she didn't want anything from the snack counter.

She stopped to stare out a window for a few minutes and then headed back. Suddenly, nothing seemed familiar. She looked at the signs at the next corner and found herself in the pediatrics wing.

Nick's room was the other way. She turned around and came face to face with a preteen girl pulling an IV pole along, her bright pink robe covered with penguins.

Whitney stopped short. "I'm sorry. I realized I was headed the wrong way. I didn't know you were behind me."

"That's okay." The girl draped her arm around the control box of her rolling companion. "I'm only doing my laps. I have to walk around this loop three times twice a day." She pointed down the hall and around the corner, circling the unseen connecting hallway and back to where they stood. "If I'm strong enough, they may let me go home on Christmas. Otherwise, here I'll be with the other sicko kids."

"Your parents aren't with you?"

"They come to visit, but we live a hundred miles from here, and Mom's got three younger ones at home. Dad took all his vacation to be with me for doctor visits and my surgery." She shrugged. "It's not a big deal, but I would like to be home for Christmas."

"Of course. I hope you can."

Following the signs toward Nick's room, Whitney stopped at a small chapel. The room stood empty and peaceful. Thoughts of the girl in the pajamas and her talk with Carol swirled in her head. Then her father's words of apology came to her. A wave of gratitude flowed through her for all she had, and her plans for the perfect Christmas melted away in the face of the things that really mattered.

Nick was waking when she returned, and the nurse who wanted the picture of her daughter came by soon after to confirm her order.

After she left, Whitney entertained Nick with stories of crazy craft store customers while she finished Trish's picture. He, in turn, told her what he'd learned about the night nurse. "She's going to medical school during the day and works nights to pay for it. I don't know when she sleeps."

Whitney added a few things to the blessings she'd been counting. "I can't imagine living that way all the time. You know what a grump I've been these last couple of weeks with less sleep."

"No comment." He grinned at her.

A middle-aged nurse stepped into the room. "It's time for your sponge bath and clean sheets." She smiled at Whitney. "You can stay if you want, but this is a good time to run errands."

Very diplomatic, Whitney thought. "I'll give you the room." She kissed Nick goodbye. "Is there anything you need? I have to go home to frame these pictures before I deliver them."

"I'd like my laptop. There's Wi-fi, so I can check emails and keep up with the office memos."

"Okay, but you worry about healing, not work." She waved goodbye and headed for the parking lot.

Once home, she got out of the car and walked toward the front door. Something seemed wrong.

She stepped onto the grass and gazed at the house. The string of lights no longer dangled from the eaves but hung neatly in place. A note on the door included well wishes from the Yeagers across the street. They'd seen the ambulance and figured out what had happened. Mr. Yeager had finished the job. They wished the Saunders a Merry Christmas despite the accident.

What a thoughtful thing her neighbors had done. Her previous ungenerous reaction to the impulse to deliver Christmas goodies weighed on her. It wasn't too late. She'd make up a plate of goodies out of the freezer and take it over before she left. She unlocked the door with a smile on her face.

Inside, the Christmas decorations brought back a tinge of sadness. What if they couldn't spend Christmas at home? She looked at the tree with its menagerie of stuffed animals they had so carefully arranged. A large penguin near the bottom had fallen askew, and she reached out to straighten it.

As she touched it, she thought of the girl with the penguin robe at the hospital. She'd said there were other kids who would be spending Christmas there. The blessings she'd been counting all morning swirled around in her mind. She laughed as she remembered Carol's words. "You can only make the best of what comes along. Some of my most treasured memories are from when my plans fell completely apart."

It was time to make a new plan.

She ran to the kitchen and grabbed a garbage bag. Back at the tree, she snatched off the toys and stuffed them into the bag as quickly as she could. She had a lot to do, and she didn't want to be gone long.

She stowed the bag in the trunk of the car and raced back inside to make up a large plate of goodies. Then she got out a tray and filled it with most of the rest of the stash. She grabbed two of her leftover Christmas cards to include with the treats. She wrote a note to the neighbors on one and to the staff at the hospital on the other. To the Yeagers, she said, "Thank you for being part of our village."

She framed the pictures she'd made for her coworkers and wrapped them, attaching the last three Christmas cards. On the way out the door, she remembered Nick's laptop and went back for it. Once everything was piled in the car, she fished the business card out of her purse and called Santa to change her arrangement with him.

At Whit's End ~ 13

NICK SEEMED FULLY awake and anxious to see her when she finally entered Room 205. "Hey, gorgeous."

She rushed to his side. "I've hijacked your Christmas." She took his hand and explained about the goodies and Santa, keeping only his stocking in reserve for Christmas day. "I took all the animals off our tree. I called Santa and asked him to come to the pediatrics unit on Christmas Eve instead of our house. He's not even going to charge extra. The nurses will gather the children for his visit." She took a deep breath and continued. "The neighbors finished putting up the lights, so I gave them a plate of cookies. The rest are in the staff room for your nurses except the few I left in the freezer for your homecoming." She stopped and peered into his eyes. "What do you think?"

He pulled her into a hug. "I think I love you."

ᏣᏉ

On Christmas Eve, Whitney wheeled Nick into a corner of the pediatric waiting room at 6:15. Children arrived in wheelchairs, pulling IV poles, or supported by parents and nurses.

At 6:30 exactly, Santa appeared lugging an overstuffed bag. "Ho, ho, ho, look at all these good little boys and girls." His eyes roamed the room. Then he strode over to the girl in the pink robe. He pulled the penguin from the top of the bag and wished her a Merry Christmas. She thanked him then smiled at Whitney.

Santa talked with each child, pulling out a stuffed animal and presenting it at the end of each visit. Then he asked if there were any children who had to remain in bed. One of the nurses led him down the hall, and the children filed out behind them.

Nick reached for his wife's hand. "I think you found our very own Christmas tradition. Let's do this every year."

"Absolutely, but I do have one more surprise for you." She came around in front of his wheelchair. "The doctor says you can go home tomorrow."

"Great!" Nick's face took on a mischievous look. "I have a Christmas surprise for you, too. One of those emails you didn't want me looking at included our insurance documents. Our health insurance took effect the day before my accident."

"That's not only a surprise—it's a Christmas miracle." Whitney gazed at her broken husband through misty eyes. "We get to spend the holiday together in our own home with our naked tree and a little plate of goodies."

Nick beamed up at her. "That's my idea of a perfect Christmas."

About Terry Deighton

Terry Deighton lives in Sedro-Woolley, Washington with her husband, Al. Occasionally, one or another of their six grown children pop in to visit, making life interesting. When she's not substitute teaching, writing, or editing, she loves to Skype with her grandchildren, read, and hang out in her husband's woodshop. At least she wants him to think she loves it. She also loves Christmas. Her first-hand knowledge of how to make too much of a good thing earned her the nickname, The Grumpy Santa.

Made in the USA
Charleston, SC
14 December 2014